MINE
TO TAKE

CYNTHIA
EDEN

For my readers...THANK YOU so much for supporting my work! I hope that you enjoy this romantic suspense tale!

PROLOGUE

Blood dripped into her eyes. Pain rolled through her body, and she tried to fight it, tried to break free, but she couldn't.

Trapped.

The metal had twisted around her. It held her in a grip too tight and too hard, and every move she made just caused her to hurt even more.

She screamed for help, but no one was there to save her.

The rain poured down, pelting through the broken windshield. Her car had rolled, again and again, down the incline. Would anyone from the road even be able to see her?

"I'm here!" She screamed again.

Every part of her body hurt. Broken glass was all around her. The blood and rain mixed together on her face.

She begged for help until her voice broke.

Until the rain stopped.

Until the pain finally stopped.

There was nothing left, nothing but the darkness.

It was in that darkness that she heard his voice.

"I'm here...I've got you..."

And when she heard him, she was afraid.

CHAPTER ONE

Skye Sullivan stared up at the building before her. It shot high into the sky, its massive windows gleaming in the light. There were too many floors for her to count. Looking more like a fortress than an office, the place spoke of power.

And money. A lot of it.

"Miss?" The doorman eyed her with a hint of concern in his dark eyes.

Probably because she was standing in the middle of the street, gawking up at the place. Skye gave a quick shake of her head, pulled her coat a bit closer around her, and hurried inside that fortress. Getting out of that icy Chicago air was a relief for her.

Another man waited behind the gleaming desk in the lobby. She glanced to the left and the right, and Skye nervously noted the security cameras that followed her every move.

Cautiously now, she approached the desk. "I, um, I'm looking for Trace Weston."

The man, in his early twenties and sporting a stylish blue suit, raised his brows at her. "Do you have an appointment?"

Not exactly. She'd barely gathered the courage to actually head into this place. Twice that morning, she'd turned around and almost gone back to her home.

I need him.

Skye straightened her shoulders. "No, I don't have an appointment."

His eyes narrowed.

She rushed on, saying, "My name is Skye Sullivan, and I-I'm an...old friend of his." Okay, so that part that wasn't exactly the truth.

But she was desperate. No, more than that. She was scared.

When she'd done a search looking for private detectives in the area, Weston Securities had immediately popped up on her computer screen. As soon as she'd seen the name, Skye's whole body had tensed.

Trace Weston. Some men left a mark on a woman, a mark that went far beneath the skin.

Trace had marked her years before.

His company was way out of her price range, Skye got that. The lobby even smelled expensive. And, after the accident, pretty much *everything* was out of her range, but she didn't have a choice.

She had to get Trace to help her.

Besides, they *had* been friends once.

Before they'd been lovers. Before everything had gone to hell.

The guy in the fancy suit looked down at his computer. "I don't think you understand just how busy Mr. Weston's schedule is, ma'am. If you'd like to speak with one of the junior associates here, I'm sure that we can find someone available."

Her heartbeat thudded in her ears. A junior associate. Right. Well, that was certainly better than nothing.

The phone on the man's desk rang. "Excuse me," he murmured as he reached for the phone.

Skye nodded. Her cheeks were burning. Had she really thought that she could get Trace to help her? That she could just walk into this place and he'd be there for her? After all the time that had passed, she'd be lucky if the guy even remembered her.

If only I could have forgotten him.

"Y-yes, sir. Right now." A sharp note of nervousness had entered the man's voice.

Skye glanced back at him as he hurriedly put the phone down. His eyes, a warm gray, had come back to her. Now there was some definite curiosity in his stare. "You're to go right up, Ms. Sullivan." He pushed a clipboard toward her. "Sign in first, then I'll take you to the elevator."

Her gaze slid to the nearest security camera. Tension tightened her shoulders as she scribbled her name across the page. Then Skye hurried toward the elevators on the right. *Don't limp. Don't. Take slow steps. Nice and slow.*

"Not that elevator." He caught her elbow and steered her to the left. "This one." He pulled a keycard from his pocket. Swiped it across the elevator's panel. The doors opened almost instantly, and he guided Skye inside. "Go up to the top floor. Mr. Weston will be waiting for you."

But Mr. Weston hadn't even known she was coming to the building. "I don't understand —" Skye began.

The doors slid closed.

Her hands trembled as the elevator shot up. The elevator's walls were made of glass and she turned, glancing out at the view of the city.

A lot could change for a person in ten years. You could go from having absolutely nothing...to having everything.

Or you could go from everything...*to nothing.*

The elevator slowed. Skye turned back toward the doors. She took a deep breath. Then those doors slid open.

Her shoes sank into lush carpet as she stepped out of the elevator.

"Ms. Sullivan?"

She glanced over at the pretty blonde woman who'd rushed toward her.

The blonde smiled. "This way, please."

Trace had seen her on the video cameras. That was the only explanation. He'd seen her, and he'd actually remembered her.

Well, you were always supposed to remember your first, weren't you?

He'd been her first. Once upon a time, he'd been her everything.

The blonde opened a gleaming, mahogany door. "Ms. Sullivan is here, sir."

Don't limp. Skye stepped inside the office and saw him.

The man who'd haunted her.

The man who'd taught her about lust and loss.

Trace Weston.

He sat behind a massive desk. He'd leaned back in his chair, and his head was tilted to the right as his eyes — still the bluest that she'd ever seen — swept over her body. His hair was midnight black, cut to perfectly frame the strong planes of his face.

Handsome wasn't a word that could be used to describe Trace. It never had been. *Sexy. Dangerous.* Those were words for him.

The door shut behind Skye, sealing her inside the office with him.

Trace rose from his seat. He came toward her, his stride slow and certain. With every step that he took, she tensed, her body helpless to do otherwise.

"H-hello, Trace." She hated that stupid break in her voice. Trace made her nervous. Always had.

He stopped in front of her. He stood at several inches over six feet, while she barely skimmed five feet three. Skye tilted her head back so that she could meet his stare.

"It's been a long time," Trace said, the words a deep, dark rumble. His voice went perfectly with the rock hard body and the sexy face — a voice that a woman could imagine in the darkness.

She swallowed because her throat was suddenly dry. "Yes, it has." Ten years and three months. Not that she'd counted.

That assessing gaze of his slid down her body once more. There was an awareness in his stare that she hadn't expected. A heat that made her remember too many things.

He was close enough to touch. Close enough for her to smell the crisp, masculine scent that clung to him.

His nostrils flared, as if he were catching her scent, too.

"You look good, Skye." Again, that heat was in his stare. A heat that said he knew her intimately.

She wished her heartbeat would slow down.

"But you're not here for a friendly chat, are you?" And he stepped away from her. He waved to the open chair near his desk and returned to his seat.

"We've never really been the friendly chat kind," she said softly as she eased into the leather chair.

She didn't take off her coat. She just pulled it closer to her.

A faint furrow appeared between his brows. "No, we weren't, were we? More the hot sex type."

Her lips parted. He had *not* just said that to her.

His faint smile said that he had.

"I'm not here for that, *either*." She'd been wrecked after her last go round with Trace.

He leaned back in his chair. The leather groaned beneath him. "We'll get to that…"

Uh, *no*, they wouldn't. She wasn't ready to feel that burn again.

He tapped his chin. "You're not here for pleasantries, you're not here for sex, then why have you come looking for me?"

This was where she'd have to beg. Because there was *no* way she had enough money in her account to cover his services. Not with the guy sporting this high rise building and looking like he'd just walked off the cover of *GQ*. *How things have changed.* "Someone is watching me."

He stilled. The heat banked in his eyes as his whole expression instantly became guarded. "And what makes you so sure of that?"

"Because I can feel him." Wait, that sounded crazy, didn't it? When she'd gone to the cops, they'd sure looked at her as if she were crazy. You couldn't *feel* a stalker. So they said.

She disagreed.

Trace wasn't speaking.

So she did the talking, saying quickly, "I know someone has been watching me, okay? When I go to my studio, when I go out at night…" A tenseness would slip over her. An awareness that was instinctive.

"You *think* someone is following you."

He wasn't believing her any more than the cops had. "I *think,*" she stressed the word back to him as her hands clenched, "that someone has been in my house. Things are rearranged. They aren't where I put them. My doors are locked but someone has been getting in."

Now he leaned forward. "What's been rearranged?"

"Cl-clothes."

His piercing stare stayed on her face.

"Underwear," she whispered. "Some panties are missing. Some…some are left on my bed."

"Fuck."

Yes, that was exactly how she felt. "Cops aren't buying my *feelings.* They don't see any signs of a break-in at my apartment. And they think I just lost my laundry."

But she knew something else was happening.

She licked too dry lips. "This…this isn't the first time this has happened."

His hands had flattened on his desk.

"When I was in New York…" That seemed like a life-time away. "The same thing was happening before my accident. Someone would get into my apartment." At first, the whole thing had started harmlessly enough. *Just with flowers.* "He started by leaving flowers in my dressing room." She'd gone into her dressing room after a performance and found them waiting for her. No note. Just the flowers.

Trace waited for her to continue.

Her chest ached as she said, "The next time I found the flowers, they were in my apartment. My *locked* apartment."

A muscle flexed along his jaw. "And you're sure the flowers weren't just a gift from a lover?"

"I don't have a lover." She shook her head. "Not then. Not now."

What she had was someone who was terrifying her. A shadow that seemed to follow her wherever she went. "I came here because I was hoping that one of your agents might be able to help me. That you could assign someone to follow-up and just *see* what's happening."

His gaze seemed to bore into her. She'd always felt like Trace saw too deeply when he looked at her.

But she couldn't look away. "The police won't help me. I was hoping that you could." Skye kissed her pride good-bye. When this much fear was involved, there was no room for pride. She had secrets that she wasn't telling him, not yet. *"Please,* Trace. I need you."

"You have me." Said instantly.

Her breath eased out. "Thank you." *Tell him about the money.* "Maybe we can — we can work out some kind of payment plan —"

"Screw the money." He rose from his desk again. Stalked toward her. Her head tilted back and her hair slid over her arm as she looked up at him.

He reached for her hand. Pulled her to her feet. At his touch—just that one touch—awareness poured through her. Heat flushed her cheeks. Memories tightened her body. That was the way it had always been between them. One touch and—

"It's still there," Trace gritted out as his hold tightened on her hand. "And we'll be getting to that, soon enough."

The dark words were a promise.

"But right now, I want to find out what the hell is going on in your life."

So did she.

***

Skye Sullivan. Skye Fucking Sullivan. The girl who'd starred in every teenage fantasy that he'd ever had. The woman who'd made him realize just how dark and wild lust could burn.

She'd come back to him. Walked straight into his building. Into his life.

He'd seen her image on the security screen. One look, and everything had changed.

She's back.

This time, things would end differently for them. He'd never had his fill of Skye.

This time, she needs me.

They stepped outside of his building. The sounds of the city instantly filled his ears—horns, voices, the backfire of engines. Skye eased away from him, heading for the cab at the corner of the street.

He caught her arm and pulled her right back against him. "We'll take my car." He'd already called for his driver. The sleek, black ride was waiting to the right. The driver—who doubled as one of Trace's guards—held the back door open for them.

"We'll be heading to Skye's apartment," Trace murmured to Reese Stokes.

Skye hesitated, then quickly rattled off the address.

Reese nodded. Reese had been with Trace for over five years now, and Trace trusted the man implicitly.

Skye slid into the vehicle first, and when she did, her skirt lifted, revealing a silken expanse of leg covered in nylon.

Once upon a time, Skye had enjoyed wearing thigh-highs. He'd bought them for her. Because he'd loved the feel of them against her skin.

She disappeared into the car.

Eyes narrowing, memories swirling through his mind, Trace followed her. The door shut, sealing them inside. The privacy shield was already in place, completely blocking them from Reese's scrutiny.

The car pulled away from the curb.

"I thought one of your agents would handle this. I mean, you're the boss." Her words came a little too quickly. She'd always done that. Spoken fast when she was nervous.

It's good that I still make her nervous.

"I'm sure you don't have time to spend on me."

On the contrary. He slid back into the seat next to her, making sure that their shoulders brushed. "You're not going back to New York."

Her head jerked toward him. Her eyes—deep, dark green—met his. There was gold in her eyes, buried in the green. When she was aroused, the gold burned hotter.

And when she was aroused, her cheeks flushed, her fuck-me lips trembled, and a moan would slip from her lips.

Skye Sullivan. Porcelain perfect. So delicate that he'd once worried his passion might bruise her.

He still worried because the things he wanted from her...

I'm not a boy any longer.

He'd already held back with her for too long.

Her dark hair fell down her shoulders, long and silken. When she danced, she kept her hair pinned up, making her cheekbones look even sharper.

When she danced…

She made him ache.

"There's nothing for me in New York any longer." Her voice was stilted. Not Skye. Skye spoke with humor and life. But when she'd come into his office, finally come back to him, there had been fear in her voice—and in her eyes. "I was in an…accident."

"I know." The story had been all over the news. The prima ballerina who'd been trapped in the wreckage of her car on a storm filled night. She'd danced for thousands, she'd lit up the stages in New York.

And she'd barely survived that crash.

He forced air into his lungs. *Don't think about it. She's here.*

"I've had physical therapy on my leg." Said with grim pride as her chin—slightly pointed—came into the air. "I can dance, just not like…not like before." She gave a little shake of her head. "The stage won't be for me any longer."

"That's why you came home?"

Home. The only home he'd ever had—it had been with her.

Two foster kids. Tossed through the system again and again. He'd met her when he was seventeen. She'd been fifteen.

"That's why I came back to Chicago," she agreed, voice husky. "I'm saving money to open a studio. I'll teach here. I can still do that."

Her dancing had gotten her out of poverty. Into the bright lights of studios and stages in New York. Her dancing had given her a new life.

And taken her from his.

"The money is a problem." She wasn't looking at him anymore. He wanted her eyes on his.

He leaned toward her. Caught her hand.

That made her gaze fly right back to his. "I'll find a way to pay you," she told him. "I can do it, just give me some time."

His going rate—for his newest junior agents, not for his personal services because he didn't go into the field any longer—was three hundred an hour. "We'll work it out."

He had plenty of plans for her.

His fingers threaded through hers. His hand swallowed hers. His skin was rough and dark, tanned from the time he spent in the sun. Her hand was pale, almost fragile. So very breakable.

Hadn't he always thought that about her? From the first moment he'd seen her, when he'd rushed into that room, hearing her scared cries…

Don't, please don't!

She'd been his to save then.

His.

"What are you thinking about?" Skye whispered.

"The way it used to be."

Her lashes were long. Her dark green eyes were so sexy. Her breath slipped out a little too quickly. "I wasn't sure you'd even remember me."

Only every damn minute. There were some things a man could never forget.

"You should have come to me sooner." He hated to think of her out there, afraid.

Alone.

"The last time we spoke," her voice seemed to stroke right over him, "you told me to get the hell out of your life. Coming back wasn't easy."

The car slowed.

His jaw had locked. *You're not getting away so easily this time.*

"I think we're here," she said and tugged on her hand.

He didn't release her. "You said you didn't have a lover." Good. He didn't want to think of her with some other bastard.

Her gaze held his.

"You will, Skye."

She shook her head. "Trace…"

His name was a husky murmur from her. Denial and need all tied together.

Her lips were too close. She smelled too good. Sweet vanilla. Good enough to damn well eat.

He took her mouth. Not gently. Not softly. Because he'd never been that kind of guy. Trace knew he wasn't the tender lover type.

He'd fought for every single thing that he had. He'd keep fighting.

His tongue thrust into her mouth. She tasted even sweeter than she smelled. Her lips were soft and lush, and she was kissing him back. A low moan rose in her throat, and her tongue slid lightly against his.

He'd been the one to teach her how to kiss.

And to fuck.

He deepened the kiss, needing more, so much more from her than he could get right then. She'd come to him because she was afraid, but he wasn't interested in her fear. He wanted her passion. He wanted *her.*

She pulled back. Her lips were wet and red from his mouth.

His addiction. The one that he'd never been able to ditch.

No matter how much money he got, no matter how many women came into his bed, Skye was the one he wanted, the one that he would have.

There was a price for everything in this world. He knew that lesson well.

Skye would pay a price.

So would he.

It was a good thing he could afford that price this time.

She nearly jumped from the car when he let her go. He exited slowly, far too aware of the ache for her — and of the arousal that wasn't going away.

Sunlight glinted down on him. Early spring, but still cold because that was the way of his city. He ignored the chill and stared up at the apartment complex. Older, in a more rundown area just outside of the city.

When she'd been in New York, her place had been so much bigger — so close to the lights of Broadway.

The hospital bills had taken a lot of her money. He knew that. He knew so much more than she realized.

"Stay here," he told Reese and then Trace followed Skye to the building. Security at her apartment was non-existent. Anyone could walk right in…

And they did.

"I'm on the third floor," Skye said.

The top floor.

"The elevator is getting fixed right now, so…" She turned for the stairs.

He didn't move. "Can your leg handle that climb?"

Her shoulders snapped up. Ah, there it was. Her fierce pride. One of the things that had so drawn him to her. "Yes. I can handle it." And she didn't look back as she started on the stairs. But he noticed she clung a little too tightly to the banister.

He followed behind her, easily closing the distance that separated them, and he stayed one stair behind her, all the way up.

His gaze noted everything. The peeling paint on the walls. The lights that flickered. The lights that weren't on at all.

Sonofabitch.

Then they were on the third floor. There were three other doors on that floor, but she took him to apartment 301. He stopped her before she could put her key in the lock. Trace bent, inspecting the old, golden lock. No scratch marks to indicate that someone had tried to pick it. There were no signs of tampering at all.

He eased back. She unlocked the door. It opened with a groan of sound, the hinges ancient and obviously in need of oil. Skye hurried inside, stumbling just a little, before she flipped on the lights.

The apartment was small but so very Skye. Bright colors lit the walls, comfortable furniture filled the interior. The curtains were pulled back near the windows, letting the light spill inside.

The place smelled of her.

He advanced toward the windows. The fire escape led all the way up to her floor. The windows were locked there, and, again, he didn't see any sign of tampering.

"I know what you're doing." She stood a few feet behind him. "The detective—Griffin—didn't find any sign of a break-in, either. But I'm telling you, someone has been here."

"Did I say that I didn't believe you?" He glanced back at her.

Skye shook her head.

"Take me to your bedroom."

She rocked back a step.

"That's where he goes, doesn't he?" Trace didn't let any emotion enter his voice. Now wasn't the time for emotion.

Skye spun away and walked down the narrow hallway. She opened another door. "It's...here."

He brushed past her and stepped inside the small room. The bed was wooden, an old four-poster. A chest of drawers—one that had been painted a bright blue—waited to the left. A matching dresser stood to the right.

Nothing looked disturbed in her room. "When is the last time you think he was here?"

"Last night," she said as her gaze went to the bed. "When I came home last night, my—my underwear was left on the bed."

He stared at the bed.

"I didn't leave them there," she continued, voice tight. "I know I didn't. Someone is playing some kind of game with me."

"I don't think it's a game." Trace glanced away from the bed and back at her. Skye hadn't moved away from the door. "I think someone is stalking you." He paused. "Someone like this can be very, very dangerous."

Her eyes were on his.

"To break into your home, to follow you…" He lifted his hand and brushed back the hair that had slipped over her shoulder. "It sounds like the guy is fixated on you."

"You'll find him, though?"

"I will. My agents will watch your place. No one will get in here again."

Her breath whispered out. "Thank you."

"I'll get better locks on your doors and windows." He'd do a hell of a lot more than that. "You'll be safe here."

She nodded quickly.

"You'd be safer…" He had to say it. "If you came back home with me."

Her eyes widened. "Trace…"

"It's not like it would be the first time, Skye."

She retreated. Her back hit the door frame. "No. I didn't come to you…for *that*."

That. The storm of lust and need and want that had consumed them before.

The uncontrolled desire had almost destroyed them both.

"I need your help, Trace, but that's all."

It wasn't all he wanted. But he'd give her this moment. Soon enough, she'd be coming to him.

I know her weaknesses.

Trace inclined his head. "Then I'll get your protection started. It's the least I can do for my old…friend." Once more, his body brushed past hers. The tension rolled off her as he headed into the hallway.

"We were, once."

Her voice halted him.

"We were friends before we were anything more." Her words were soft, like a whispered confession.

Yes, they had been friends, but they'd lost that, long ago.

He pulled out his phone even as he headed for the front door. As soon as the front door closed, he demanded, "I want agents at Skye Sullivan's apartment." The address came from him as a curt bark. "New locks. A video camera and alarm inside." She didn't even *have* an alarm. "I want a team watching the place." He remembered the way her hand had gripped the banister. "And I want the fucking elevator fixed."

His orders would be obeyed. His staff jumped at his command. He wasn't the abandoned, penniless kid anymore. He had the power now.

Trace glanced over his shoulder at Skye's closed apartment door.

He had the power, and he was going to use it.

***

The dream came again. It snuck up on him when he was tired or when *she* got into his mind too much.

He found himself back in that old house. The one with the roof that sagged. With carpets that had been worn bare.

Another home. Another place.

His first night there.

"Don't, please…"

The voice had called out to him.

He'd been on his feet before he'd thought twice. On his feet and on his way to *her*.

The dream took over.

His fist shoved open the wooden door, revealing a small bedroom. He hadn't seen that one when they'd brought him in to the house earlier that day. Two people were on the bed. The boy — his new "brother" Parker. The other was the girl…the one with the long hair and the sad eyes.

The pretty girl who'd been too shy to speak to him before.

But he was sure her voice had been the one calling to him, begging, "Please, don't…"

Only she wasn't speaking anymore. Wasn't crying out, not pleading.

Because Parker had his hand over her mouth.

"What the hell are you doing?" Trace demanded.

"Get out, man, get out!" Parker snapped back, but he kept his voice low.

So his parents wouldn't hear?

Trace's gaze shot to the girl. Tears leaked from her eyes. Parker had one hand over her mouth, and one of his hands pinned her small wrists to the bed.

Rage pushed through Trace. "Get off her, now."

"Get out," Parker said again, "or I'll tell my parents to ship your ass out of here. This is my *house, I say what — "*

He didn't get to say anything else. Trace knocked the guy off her. He drove his fist into Parker's face, again and again. Bones broke. Blood spurted. Trace kept hitting him.

"Stop! You're going to kill him!" Her voice. Her hands on him.

Trace's eyes flew open as the dream — his past — vanished.

His hands were clenched into fists.

Skye needed him again.

I won't let her down.

CHAPTER TWO

Skye stared at her reflection. Too pale. Too thin. She didn't look like a star who belonged in the center of the lights.

That's not who I am.

Sometimes, she wasn't sure she'd ever really been that woman.

Her hands reached for the barre. She'd installed it herself. Just gotten the mirrors positioned a few moments ago. Right after she'd finished up the paint job. Done it all—herself. There was a grim pride in her accomplishment. She'd sweated blood and tears for this place.

The studio had taken the last of her money. She'd put down her deposit and paid rent for a half a year. Skye knew that opportunity—that precious six months—was her chance. To do something. To get her life back.

The studio was hers. She *would* make it work.

Only the image staring back at her in the mirror didn't look so certain.

Skye rose onto her toes, ignoring the twinge in her left calf. That twinge would soon turn to an ache, but she'd ignore that, too. She'd grown used to ignoring pain over the years. That was the first rule of dancing. *No pain.* If your body was weak, you ignored the weakness. You danced until your feet bled. Then you went out onto the stage, and you danced some more.

Her arms stretched. Her back arched. Her first dance class would start in three days. That would give her just enough time to—

The lights turned off. Every single light shut off at once, plunging her into total darkness.

Her heels hit the hardwood floor. *The circuit breaker.* Dammit, this same problem had happened before. Only then it had been daytime and sunlight had trickled through the windows, providing enough illumination for her to see. Now, there was just night to deepen the darkness.

She kept her hand on the barre as she made her way to the door. The building manager had promised her that the problem had been fixed.

This isn't fixed. This is—

A faint rustle of sound reached her ears.

Like a shoe. The quick press of a footstep.

Skye froze. "Is...is someone there?" When she'd left her apartment, Trace's men had been installing new locks and an alarm system. One of the men had even followed her to the dance studio. She was supposed to be safe.

The floor squeaked. She knew that squeak. There was a weak spot near the front door. Every time she came inside the studio, she stepped in that spot and the floor squeaked beneath her.

Not alone.

She stopped advancing toward the door. Instead, she backed up, fast.

"Skye..." A rasp of her name.

Turning, she ran away from that rasp.

But she didn't get far. Hard hands grabbed her and locked tight around her stomach. He spun her around and jerked her against his body—and those hands holding her so tightly *hurt*.

"*I've been watching...*" His voice was still a rasp. A terrifying rasp. He was bigger than she was. So much bigger and stronger, and he held her easily when she twisted against him.

But he hadn't covered her mouth. His mistake. *"Help me!"* She screamed as loudly as she could.

Trace's agent was outside. He'd hear her. He'd —

Her attacker slammed her into the mirror. The glass cracked and shattered around her. His fingers pressed over her mouth, reminding her of a nightmare from her past that wouldn't ever stop.

Her head ached where it had hit the mirror. The wooden barre shoved into her back.

His breath blew against the shell of her ear. "I will be the one," he told her, voice low and hard.

She lifted her knee. Tried to shove it into his groin, but he was already pulling back.

Even as the sound of footsteps pounded toward her.

Footsteps — and a light?

"Ms. Sullivan?"

She clung to the barre. It seemed to be the only thing holding her up right then. *He was here. He was here.*

The flashlight hit her in the face. "Ms. Sullivan, what happened? I heard you cry for help." It was her guard — Reese Stokes. She recognized his deep voice and that faint Alabama accent. If she could have moved, Skye would have hugged that man right then. Instead, she managed to say, "He's here!"

That flashlight immediately swept the room, cutting through the darkness. But finding no one.

"He?" Reese asked her as he came closer. He put his arm around her.

"He's here," Skye said again. Trace had warned her, he'd told her…*He's dangerous.* He'd been right. If Reese hadn't been there, what would her attacker have done?

"Skye?"

At that familiar, deep voice, she tensed in Reese's arms. *Trace.*

The lights flooded back on at that moment, coming with a brightness that almost hurt her eyes.

Trace rushed toward her. He pulled her from Reese. "What the hell just happened?"

"She said someone was here." Reese seemed to have just noticed the broken glass.

"Go. Search," Trace ordered as he pulled Skye even closer to him. "I've got her."

Pieces of the broken mirror had fallen to the floor. They crunched beneath Trace's expensive shoes.

Reese hurried away from them. When he ran away, Skye saw the gun in his hand.

Her breath choked out. *Why is this happening?*

Trace's fingers slid through her hair. He growled, "Dammit, you could have a concussion."

What she had was a giant knot on her head. One that was making her dizzy and nauseous. Wait, was that a concussion?

"I'm getting you out of here."

Before she could say anything else, he'd lifted her into his arms. He held her easily, as if she weighed nothing at all, and he hurried for the door.

Then they were outside. The crisp air hit her, pushing back some of the nausea, but not doing a thing to alleviate her fear. The fear had far too tight of a grip on her.

Trace carried her toward a dark Jag. He opened the door and sat her inside on the passenger's seat. "Tell me what happened."

She hadn't seen him in ten years. So why was she so ridiculously glad that *he* was the one there with her? "I was practicing…the lights went out. I-I thought it as the breaker. It's gone out before and—"

He caught her chin in his hand. "When did the man come?"

She swallowed. "When it went dark. I heard the floor squeak, and I knew he was there." She licked her too-dry lips. "I tried to run, but he caught me."

"Did he…" Trace's words were gritted, "what did he do to you?"

Her eyelids flickered as she remembered. "He slammed my head into the mirror. Reese came in…before he could do anything else."

I will be the one.

Her hands were shaking. She balled them into fists in her lap.

"I'm taking you to the hospital."

"No, I—"

"I'm *taking* you to the hospital," Trace said again, anger snapping in the words. "You've got a concussion. You need to be checked out."

"Boss!" Reese rushed toward them. "I searched the building, but no one's there."

Her gaze darted down the street. There were other buildings, a few shops nearby, but they were all closed for the night.

"Stay here. Get back-up on the scene," Trace ordered Reese. "I want that SOB. And we're getting him."

Then he slammed her door shut. She watched him through the window, chill bumps rising on her skin. Trace leaned close to Reese. Whispered something that she couldn't hear. The chill bumps got worse. Skye felt so cold then. So very cold.

Trace turned away from Reese and stalked back toward her. The driver's door opened. Trace slid inside the vehicle, and the engine growled to life.

I will be the one.

The words wouldn't stop whispering through her mind.

The car's engine snarled to life, and the Jag shot into the night.

She looked back. Reese stood there, staring after them. Her studio was lit up, every light glowing.

And the monster who'd been in the dark—he was long gone.

But he'll be back.

The cold sank down, penetrating all the way to her bones.

***

"Definitely concussed," the doctor said as she shone a light into Skye's eyes.

Trace crossed his arms over his chest. He'd moved back so the doctor could work on Skye, but he hadn't been about to leave the small exam room. He wasn't in the mood to let Skye out of his sight.

"We'll need you to stay overnight for observation," Dr. Denise Bond told Skye as she lowered her light. "It's a precaution in a situation like this—"

"No," Skye said, her immediate denial cutting through the doctor's words. "I'm going home."

"I don't think you realize how dangerous a concussion could be." The doctor spoke carefully, still in that soothing bedside manner that some docs managed so easily. "Brain injuries are unpredictable. Your concussion appears mild now, but what if you have a seizure in the middle of the night? What if you fall…is there someone at your home that can help you?"

Skye's green gaze darted to Trace, then back to the doctor. "I-I'll be fine."

She'll be alone.

The doctor glanced back at him.

"*I'm* the patient," Skye reminded her. Trace rather liked the snap of anger in her voice. Before, Skye had been afraid. She'd been shaking when he first rushed inside that studio.

Reese should have been taking better care of her. The agent had screwed up.

No, I screwed up. I should have kept her closer. Too much time had been wasted.

"Are you...involved with the patient?" The doctor asked him, obviously trying to figure out his relationship with Skye.

He nodded. She didn't need to know more. "She won't be alone."

Some of the tension eased from the doctor's face. "You're going to need to keep her awake. Monitor her through the night."

"Trace..." Skye began.

"Consider it done," he said.

The doctor nodded, looking grateful. "I'll go prepare discharge orders." But then she hesitated. "You will keep a close eye on her?"

"The closest possible," Trace promised.

The doctor hurried from the room, and Trace headed toward the exam table. He locked eyes with Skye. Forgot about the doctor. "This is the way it will play out. You come with me, or you spend the night here."

Bright spots of color stained her cheeks. "I've been inside hospitals long enough. After the accident, I had *weeks* of therapy. I can't stay here."

His hands pressed into the exam table on either side of her. "Then you're coming with me." She'd been the one to walk into his office. To return to him. He wasn't about back away now.

"He's accelerated," Trace told her as he leaned in close. The room smelled like antiseptic, but she smelled of sweet vanilla. He was close enough to see the gold in her eyes. "He snuck past my guard. He got to you. He hurt you." Trace barely held back his fury. "I'm not leaving you on your own until that SOB is off the streets."

A knock sounded at the door then. He glanced over his shoulder.

"This is Detective Alex Griffin!" A voice called. "Skye, I need to talk with you."

Trace's eyes narrowed. He'd been wondering when the local boys in blue would be showing up.

"He's the one who's been handling my case," Skye murmured. "The doctors...they must have called the police in."

"You were assaulted." Trace knew the notification would have been standard protocol.

"I guess he has to believe me now," she said, voice tense.

His gaze cut back to her. Skye was clad in a one of those green paper hospital gown. She looked so fragile sitting on that table. Her eyes were huge. Her hair a dark curtain around her face.

"Skye!" The detective called again.

And, before she could respond, the guy began to open the door.

Trace moved quickly so that when the door opened, he was right in the cop's path.

Alex Griffin jerked to a halt when he saw Trace. "Who the hell are you?"

Trace's brows rose as he studied the detective. In his early thirties, light blond hair, fit, and with a dark stare that heated a little too much when it peered over Trace's shoulder and focused on Skye. The guy immediately put Trace on edge. "I'm Skye's friend," he said simply, but Trace knew the other man would hear the note of possessiveness that roughened his voice.

Alex stepped around him. Seemed to focus totally on Skye. "Are you all right?"

Her smile was forced. It barely lifted her lips. "Just a bump on the head. I'll be fine."

Then the detective actually reached out to her and curled his hand around hers.

Trace tensed. What the hell kind of police work was *that?* The detective was far too cozy with Skye, especially for a guy who hadn't believed her story about a stalker.

"The attack changes things," Alex told her as his fingers skimmed over her knuckles. "This is an assault. I can get a team at—"

"My team is already at her studio," Trace said as he returned to Skye's side. The detective was still holding her hand. Still staring at Skye with far too much interest. Still pissing Trace off to an alarming degree. "But your officers are certainly welcome to join the hunt."

"Your team?" Alex repeated as his brow furrowed. Then his stare—a muddy brown—was back on Trace. "I didn't catch your name."

Because he hadn't thrown it. He did now, with pleasure. "Trace Weston." Deliberately, he took Skye's hand from the detective.

Alex backed up a step. "Weston Securities?"

"Yes."

Alex whistled and glanced back at Skye. "You hired him to keep you safe?" Before Skye could answer, Alex continued, "I don't get it. If Weston Securities was on the case, why the hell did she get hurt? Aren't you supposed to be the best in the damn area?"

His hold tightened on Skye. "If we're asking questions, I've got a few of my own...like why the hell didn't you do your job sooner? Someone has been stalking Skye for weeks." No, much longer if she'd been watched in New York.

"Because there was no evidence," Alex gritted out. "But I tried, okay? I sent extra patrols to her house. I dropped by whenever I could. I've been trying to keep an eye on her."

The guy wanted to keep more than an eye on her. That much was obvious to Trace. The detective's expression was too intense when he glanced her way. "Don't worry, detective," Trace said, his voice flat, "I'll keep an eye on her from now on."

Skye looked between them. Her lips tightened. "I just want this man caught, okay? I want him stopped!" She pulled away from Trace and slid from the exam table. When her feet hit the floor, Trace was there to brace her, just in case.

"Tell me everything that happened," Alex told her, hunching his shoulders as he leaned in closer to her.

Back the hell off. Skye didn't need the cop crowding her.

Skye had come to Trace because there hadn't been anyone else to help her. The detective didn't get to step in now and play hero.

"There isn't much to tell." The hospital gown slipped off her right shoulder and she tried to quickly pull it back into place. "I was working in my studio. The lights went off. I-I heard the creak of the floor and knew someone was there. I tried to run, but h-he caught me."

Trace had locked his back teeth while she spoke. *Bastard, I'm going to make you pay.*

"He?" Alex pounced on that word choice. "You're sure it was a man?"

"I couldn't see him." Her stare darted to Trace. "But I could feel him. He was strong, and he was big…about Trace's height. His body curved over mine when he—he held me against him." Her voice broke a little.

Trace wanted her out of that room. He wanted her in his home, where he could protect her.

"Did he say anything to you?" Alex pressed. "Did you hear any kind of accent in his voice? Did he—"

"No accent." She shook her head. Winced a little. "He was just whispering to me."

Alex stilled. "What did he say?"

"He said, 'I will be the one,'" she told them, her voice husky. She blinked quickly, as if fighting tears. "That's all he told me, okay?" Those words came out rushed. "That he'd be the one. Then Trace's agent came rushing in and—and the guy let me go."

"After he slammed your head into the glass," Trace added, the words tearing from him.

"No, actually, he slammed my head into the glass *before* he gave me his little promise." She curled her arms around her stomach. Stared up at Trace. "Please take me home," she said. "Take me home with you."

Hell, yes.

The doctor and a nurse headed into the room then. The doc glanced Trace's way. He inclined his head. "I'll make sure she's safe tonight." Every night.

He and the detective headed out while the nurse helped Skye change. Trace would have been more than happy to do that job himself—seeing Skye nude was one of his favorite things—but he needed to clear the air with the detective.

And it seemed the guy wanted to clear the air with him, too. As soon as the door closed behind them, Alex spun toward Trace. "What's your game?"

He let his brows rise. "I'm not playing a game."

"Two days ago, Skye told me that she wasn't involved with anyone. She didn't have any family in the city, no close friends..." Alex exhaled roughly as he glared at Trace. "Now you're standing here, saying you're her 'old friend' and taking her home for the night."

Yes, that was exactly what he was doing. Wasn't the detective observant? "Skye doesn't like hospitals. After her accident in New York, I think that's understandable." He didn't like to think about her accident. Didn't like to remember —

"I've heard about you, Weston."

Good for the detective. "Most people in Chicago know about me…"

"You've got money, a freaking ton of it from all accounts."

Yes, yes, he did. He'd come a long way from being the poor kid on the streets.

"And you've got dangerous connections."

"Safe connections aren't any fun," he murmured.

Alex's eyes narrowed. "You're high profile. You take the big cases. You *don't* sign on as some woman's bodyguard."

If the detective kept pushing, he'd find out just how hard Trace could push back. "This isn't some woman," Trace said. Time for his turn to talk. "This is Skye, and, I assure you, where she is concerned, I am very involved."

"You weren't two days ago," Alex fired back.

"Two days ago…" Trace exhaled slowly and fought to chain his anger. "That would have been back when you were patrolling, doing your circles around her place."

"Yes," Alex hissed. "I've been trying to protect her —"

"And now I'm here to help you do that job."

"You looked like you were here to fuck her."

The words were low, hard. *Jealous?*

Trace stepped toward the detective. The fellow was close to his height, and even though he was a cop, he had a soft look to him that told Trace this man hadn't seen nearly enough darkness in his life.

I've seen plenty.

Enough to appreciate the light that came his way.

Alex pointed his index finger at Trace. *Bad move — that's the way to get that finger broken.* "I've got a woman being stalked," Alex snapped, "an attack on her — and suddenly, I have a new guy — wait, sorry, an *'old friend'* — who has just entered the picture. Two days ago, she said that she had *no one.*"

He kept harping on the two days bit. "She has someone," Trace told him, keeping his voice flat with a monumental effort. "And until the SOB after her is caught, Skye be staying with me. So if you need to contact her," he gave him a hard smile, "come find me."

The door opened behind them. Skye was seated in a wheelchair, and she sure didn't look happy. "They said I had to go out in this thing." Her hands lightly hit the wheels. "Some kind of hospital rule."

"Liability issue," the doctor said. "I told you, it's — "

"Standard. Right." Skye's hands rose and clenched in her lap. Her frantic gaze locked on Trace. "I need to get out of here."

"Baby, I've got you."

And he did.

He moved behind the wheelchair. Pushed her carefully. The wheels spun on the chair.

"Skye!"

The detective was a dick, and he'd just snapped Trace's last nerve. Did the fellow realize that, with just one phone call, Trace could have the guy writing parking tickets? Doing traffic patrol?

Or sitting bench at desk duty?

Alex hurried around them and stopped in front of the wheelchair. "Just how long have you known Weston?"

Skye swallowed. "Since I was fifteen years old."

Alex leaned toward her. His voice dropped, but Trace heard him clearly as he said, "I asked you to tell me about any ex's that you might have in town. Someone who might have a hard time letting go…"

Skye shook her head. "Trace never had trouble letting go."

Alex's stare swept to his.

He knows.

It was easy to recognize need, lust, in another man's eyes.

Behind the cop, Trace saw Reese striding down the hallway toward them. Trace inclined his head toward the cop. "Make sure the detective has our contact information, Reese. Skye's going to be staying with me for a while."

Her head turned toward him. "But I—"

He pushed her down the hall, leaving Reese to deal with Alex.

The detective could become a problem. Trace would have to watch him, carefully.

Because no one could be allowed to interfere with his plans for Skye.

***

She should have expected the penthouse. The elevator doors opened up, and she stepped out onto the top level of the high-rise. Trace was right at her side.

"No one can get up here without passing my guards," he told her as his fingers curled around her elbow.

Right then, she was sure glad to hear about that security.

They entered the penthouse. Her gaze swept around the place. Everything looked expensive. Everything *smelled* expensive.

And the view was killer.

If she hadn't been scared to death, literally shaking apart on the inside, she would have appreciated that view more right then.

As it was, she just wanted to go someplace and collapse.

The door shut behind them. She heard the sound of the alarm engaging. Then…Trace's hands slid down her arms. Her bare arms because all she'd had to wear out of that hospital were her workout clothes. "You're safe, Skye." His words whispered into her ear.

And the fear deepened. Because she remembered *him*. The man in the dark. His mouth at her ear. His whisper.

I will be the one.

She pulled away from Trace and headed toward the big, floor to ceiling window that looked out over Chicago.

He didn't follow her.

His voice did. Trace told her, "I'm having a top-of-the-line security system installed at your studio. And a damn electrician is going in to check your lights."

She rubbed her arms. No matter what she did, she couldn't seem to shake the chill from her body. Her gaze stared out at the city. It seemed like she could see forever from this vantage.

"You don't have to drop your life for me," she made herself speak when she just wanted to stand in silence. "I'm sure having me here…in your home…it's going to cramp your style." She'd read the papers. She knew all about his many, many exploits.

Trace certainly wasn't a man living in the past.

He was too busy seducing in the present.

That was why she hadn't told Alex about him. When the detective had asked for a list of lovers in the area, anyone who might be fixated on her, Trace had been the last man to come to her mind.

He wasn't fixated on her. He'd been the one to show her to the door.

"You aren't cramping my style."

She could see her reflection in the glass. She looked lost. Carefully, Skye schooled her features before she turned back to face him. "Won't the flavor of the week mind?" She'd seen him with some blonde just last week in the variety pages—

"Fuck it if anyone minds." He'd braced his legs apart. He stood staring at her. Behind him, a fire blazed. When had he started that fire? "This isn't about anyone but you and me."

He acted as if the last ten years hadn't happened. But not once, *not once,* had he tried to contact her. *I missed you.* She wouldn't tell him that, though. She'd already broken her pride for him too many times.

He began walking toward her. His stride was slow, certain. She wanted to back up, but there was no place to go.

Sucking in a sharp breath, Skye lifted her head and stared into his eyes.

"Reese called me when he was rushing inside that studio. He'd seen the lights go dark, and he was worried. I was only five minutes away, already coming to see you, and I couldn't get there fast enough."

This wasn't the first time she'd been in trouble. Back in New York, Skye had thought for certain that she was facing death. The memory of cold rain, of constant pain, flashed through her mind.

He hadn't come to me then.

"Ten years is a long time," she said. She hated the softness of her voice. Why couldn't she act as if the past didn't matter to her? "A lot can change over all those years."

"And a lot can stay the same." His fingers curled under her jaw. "I want you just as much now as I did then. When I saw you in my office, the same need hit me. Lust tore through me the way it always does when I'm near you."

Her hands were trembling. She lifted them and put her palms on his chest. Skye wasn't sure if she wanted to pull him closer or shove him away.

"Lust was never a problem for us, though, was it?" Skye whispered. His eyes were on her mouth.

Memories of their past flashed through her mind. She could almost taste him.

"I was your first."

Heat flushed her cheeks.

"I thought about you over the years..."

His confession jolted her.

"I wondered what you were doing...who you were with..."

His gaze was still on her mouth. Still hot. Her hyperawareness of him pushed the aches and pains from her mind. "You don't get to wonder about that." Not when he'd been the one to tell her to hit the curb. *He didn't have that right.*

"There are some things you can't control." His head bent toward her. "The way I feel about you is one of those things."

She wanted his mouth. She wanted to run from him. "Trace..."

His lips feathered over hers. Not taking. Not demanding. Soft. Gentle.

"I can't have what I want tonight, I know that," his words were whispered against her lips. "But you came back to me. And you should know...that changes everything. I let you go once. You can't expect me to do that again."

Let her go? She pushed against him now. "You told me to get the hell out of your life." Skye stumbled as she hurried away from him.

"I knew what your dreams were. I wasn't going to stand in your way. You wanted the stage. You wanted to dance."

His words froze her.

She looked back at him.

"I gave you what you wanted." A muscle jerked in his jaw. "Isn't that what I've always done? Given you every damn thing that you want."

"No. You haven't." Because there was one thing she'd wanted desperately but never gotten.

The faint lines near his eyes tightened. His face was a dangerous mask in the firelight. "What did you want?"

You. He was the thing she'd wanted most, more than dancing, more than New York, more than getting out of the hell that her life had been when she'd been a teenager.

But Trace hadn't given her a choice. He'd taken her choices away.

"What. Did. You. Want?"

He was coming toward her again.

Escape.

"Where's my room?" Her gaze flew frantically around the penthouse. "I-I need to lie down."

He kept coming. "You can't sleep. I have to keep you awake. Those were the doctor's orders. She gave me a whole list of rules for you to follow."

"I won't sleep." *I need space.* She spun away from him. Her head was throbbing again. She hurried down the darkened hallway.

He was right behind her.

She threw open the first door that she saw.

Not the guest room.

This room was masculine. Filled with heavy, cherry wood furniture. A massive bed. She could even see Trace's suit coat flung on the end of the bed—

She darted back around and found him in her path. His arms were up, blocking the door.

"You have to stay where I can keep an eye on you," he told her, voice rumbling.

"Y-you agreed to find the man who is—who is—"

"Stalking you?" Trace finished. "Because that's what he's doing, Skye. He's focused on you. He started by watching you, then by sneaking into your apartment. Tonight, he took things to the next level. He came for you. He touched you —"

Her breath rushed out.

"He's dangerous. He hurt you tonight, and I won't let him hurt you again."

"I just want to rest." To stop reliving the past and the pain and *everything*.

He took her hand in his. Lead her to the bathroom. "Take off your clothes. You'll find an extra robe waiting inside."

She hesitated.

"No seduction tonight, I give you my word."

She went into the bathroom. A robe was waiting, all right. Silk. Beautiful, emerald green. Skye slipped out of her workout clothes and into the robe. She returned to him a few moments later, almost hating the feel of that silk against her skin. "I guess this got left behind by —"

"I arranged to have it brought here for you. Just like I've ordered my men to bring your clothes here. I want you to feel safe."

He'd changed while she was in the bathroom. Ditched his clothes. Now Trace wore only a pair of black pajama pants that clung low on his hips.

Her gaze darted over him. Wide shoulders. Strong chest. Way more than a six pack.

Don't go there, don't!

Trace lifted his hand toward her. "Trust me, Skye."

She did.

She put her fingers in his.

He led her to the bed. Eased her down on the mattress. Then he wrapped his body around hers. "I won't let you sleep, but I will let you rest. Stop being afraid. Nothing can hurt you here."

She wanted to believe that.

She wanted to, so badly. But there was something she hadn't told him. She'd tried to tell the police in New York, tried to tell the doctors there, but no one had believed her.

"I'll watch you through the night."

Her heart stilled at those words. It wasn't the first time he'd told her that.

The first night she'd met him, he'd told her the same thing. After Parker had—

Shut it out.

She slammed the door before the past could hit her.

But she remembered Trace's words.

That long ago night, she'd been so scared. And he'd said...

I'll watch you through the night.

Skye didn't close her eyes, but her breath came easier as Trace held her in his arms.

The illusion of safety was a lie. Deep inside, she knew it. Physically, she could trust him—he wouldn't hurt her. But there were worse things in this world than just physical pain.

Much, much worse.

***

Alex Griffin tossed his coat over his chair and keyed up his computer.

Trace Weston. Having that guy in the picture changed fuckin' everything.

Trace Weston had plenty of money. Plenty of power.

And plenty of secrets.

The man had burst onto the security scene a few years ago, seemingly coming from nowhere.

His eyes were wrong. Whenever Trace had looked at Skye, the guy's eyes had changed. There had been need in his stare, lust, anger...

Possession.

The fellow looked at Skye Sullivan as if the woman were his, when Skye had sure been singing a different story when he'd questioned her about any relationships she might have in the city.

"I heard about the attack on Ms. Sullivan," his partner said as he came toward him. Joe Harris had been a cop for twenty years. He'd seen plenty of hell on the beat during those years. His grizzled face reflected his worry. "Shit, I was sure hoping things wouldn't get that bad."

Because their hands had been tied. The woman's feelings — her gut instincts — those hadn't been enough for them to go on. And whoever had been accessing her apartment had slipped in and out without leaving any trace behind.

Except for the small signs meant to torment Skye.

Alex stared up at Joe. Light glinted off the top of his partner's shaved head. "She's got security now. *Weston Securities.*"

Joe whistled. "How much is she paying for that set-up?"

The woman's bank account was empty, so she couldn't be paying anything.

So maybe I've checked a little deeper into Skye's life than my partner realizes.

But…

When Skye Sullivan had talked to him, she'd been afraid. He hated to see fear in a woman's eyes.

"I don't think she is paying him," Alex muttered as he leaned forward and went back to typing on his keyboard. "Seems she and Trace Weston are old friends."

Bullshit. They were ex-lovers. He knew exactly what they'd been.

"I don't trust him," Alex said flatly. Skye had just looked so *breakable* at the hospital, while Trace had been too eager to get her out of there. *And away from me.*

"Be careful with him," Joe warned him. "That's not a man you want for an enemy. Hell, if he wanted, Weston could probably have your badge — and mine — with one phone call."

Alex wasn't scared of Trace Weston.

But he was determined to uncover his secrets.

CHAPTER THREE

"Tell me what happened in New York."

Skye glanced over at Trace. They were in his kitchen—a giant monstrosity that seemed to swallow them both. His cook—*he had a personal chef!*—had made them breakfast, and she'd never tasted pancakes so perfectly fluffy in her life.

Sure, at her peak in New York, she'd been able to afford some of the finer things, but she was sure realizing that Trace had flown way out of her league.

The boy she'd remembered was long gone.

She wasn't sure if she knew the man before her at all.

"Skye..."

She gulped some more orange juice. In the bright light of day, she could almost pretend that the nightmare from last night hadn't actually happened.

Almost. The ache in her head confirmed that it had been a very scary reality.

"I was in an accident," she said carefully. The chef had bustled into the other room. "My car went off the road. I was—I was trapped." *Rain. Fear. Pain.*

"For twelve hours."

Those words had her gaze jerking to his. "Y-yes. I was pinned in the car for twelve hours." The story had been splashed all over the news. The prima ballerina who'd lost everything in a tragic accident.

Only it hadn't been an accident. She was sure of that.

His jaw clenched. "There's more you aren't telling me. More than what was in the papers."

He hadn't pushed her last night. He'd held her in his arms, talked softly to her, and made absolutely certain that she stayed awake.

Now he was back to grilling her.

"You think the man was stalking you in New York…" Trace began, frowning.

"I-I believed he was, yes. Someone was getting into my dressing room." *Tell him. Tell him.* "And I thought…the night of my accident, I thought I was being followed."

Very slowly, he put down his knife. His blue eyes glittered at her. "You're just telling me this…*now?*"

"Back in New York, I told the cops. The doctors. No one believed me."

"I believe you."

She pushed away her food. "I don't remember everything about that night. I was driving away from the city. I was—" *Thinking about the past.* She cleared her throat. "I'd just left a gas station. There was a car…it seemed to follow my every turn…" The fear was easy enough to recall. "The other car's headlights were in my mirror. Flashing on and off, low beams, then high." Blinding her.

His hands gripped the edge of the table.

"I think the other car hit me." This was the part she couldn't remember, not for certain. "The headlights had lit up my whole car. I screamed—and my vehicle flew through the air." She could only recall bits and pieces after that. Fast images. Pain.

More screams.

Skye shook her head. "But the cops said there was no sign that any other vehicle was involved. They thought I must have just lost control on the wet roads."

Her appetite was gone. Even the fluffy pancakes couldn't tempt her then.

"You should have called me."

Anger stirred within her at his words. "The story made the papers, Trace. I might not be part of the mega wealthy set..." She gestured around the kitchen, "like you. But I was a pretty well-known dancer." She'd made prima ballerina status by the time she was twenty-two. Dancing had been her *life*. "Maybe...maybe *you* should have called." How many times had she lain in that bed, wishing that she would hear from him?

She rose and eased away from the table. *From him.* "I have to get back to the studio. It's opening in two days, and I'll need to get it cleaned up." She couldn't have her new students stepping on broken glass.

"It's already done."

Skye looked back at him. He'd risen. "The mirror was replaced," he said, "the glass cleaned away, and you will *not* be having any more circuit breaker trouble."

"You didn't have to—"

"I wasn't family, so they wouldn't fucking let me in that hospital."

Her head shook, an immediate denial because he couldn't be saying—

"But I found a way to you." Trace's voice was grim and hard. "I had to make sure you were going to be all right."

He was lying. He had to be. "You weren't there. You weren't in New York."

His gaze held hers, and she couldn't look away as he said, "They had you in ICU. Your doctor was a guy named Mitch Loxley."

Like it would be hard for anyone to figure out her doctor's name. It would be especially easy for Trace and his limitless resources.

"The window near your bed looked out over the hospital courtyard. The sun came through that window, rising up fast and hard, and it would hit on your face every morning. I made sure the nurses kept your blinds down because I didn't want the light to hurt you."

Her throat had dried up. A fist seemed to squeeze her heart. "When I opened my eyes, you weren't there."

His thick eyelashes flickered. "I didn't think you'd want me to be."

Her hands were fists. Her nails sank into her palms. "I don't understand you, Trace."

He smiled then, a cold, hard grin. "I know."

"What do you want from me?"

"Everything."

She backed away. "I-I have to get to the studio." She hadn't counted on this. On him. It was all too fast. Too much.

"I'll take you there."

"Fine...just...I need to go, now."

He came toward her. Always so sure of himself. So certain. "You don't need to be afraid of me. I'm the one who'll keep you safe."

She didn't know what he was. "When I went to your office the other day, I thought you might just blow me off."

His eyes narrowed at that, and she saw the spark of anger lighten his gaze. "You underestimate yourself...and your value to me."

"I don't understand you," she whispered once more.

He bent his head. His lips feathered over hers in the briefest of caresses. "You will."

***

Two guards went into the dance studio with Skye. Trace insisted on that surveillance. She wanted to get inside, she wanted to get her place ready, then she could do just that. But she would have his men with her every moment.

Trace sat in the back of his car, his gaze on the building. Maybe he shouldn't have told Skye about his trips to the hospital in New York.

But the truth would have come out, soon enough.

Especially since he planned to take her to New York within just a few hours. "The plane's ready?" Trace asked Reese. He'd opted to leave the Jag at home and have Reese do the driving today. He had plans that he needed to make, and he could multi-task better with Reese at the wheel.

"Yes, sir. The pilot's on stand-by."

"Good." He'd wait until Skye finished her work, then they'd leave.

No one else might have believed her story, but he wasn't like the others. If Skye said that she'd been forced off that road...

I want to find out what happened in New York.

And he couldn't go to the city on his own. Skye was too uncertain of him now. He'd asked for her trust, and she'd hesitated.

No, he had to keep her close.

But he also had to be very, very careful. In New York, it would be easy for him to stumble. For her to discover more about his life.

About the last ten years.

There were some things that she'd truly be better off not knowing.

***

"I need a list of your lovers," Trace told Skye when she returned to his car that evening. He'd just pulled up, seemingly at the perfect time, but she knew one of his agents must have contacted him and told Trace that she was calling it a night.

Exhaustion pulled at her, but his growled demand…

I need a list of your lovers.

"This isn't show and tell," she mumbled as she felt her cheeks flush. "I'm not asking for—"

"The detective—Griffin—was right. The man after you could be an ex. Someone who had you once, and doesn't want to let go."

She glanced out of the window. The city passed her in a blur. "It could be an ex, or it could just be some nut-job who saw me on the street. Maybe someone who even saw me dance. Sometimes, people get dancers confused with the characters we play." She'd been plenty of people, over the years. A sleeping beauty. A wicked witch. A swan. A—

"The list of your lovers will be the starting point for us. You'll find that my resources are much stronger than the detective's. I can find these men, clear them—or—"

"They aren't guilty."

The car eased to a stop. Then turned right. Reese was up in the front. She inched forward. This wasn't the way back to Trace's penthouse. Not unless Reese was taking a different route home.

"Tell me their names."

She glanced over at Trace. "They're not even in the city, okay?"

There was only one ex-lover for her in Chicago, and he was sitting far too close and taking up far too much room in the vehicle.

One dark brow rose. "It's not hard to hop a flight or a train to Chicago."

No, it wasn't.

Rain began to fall, splattering against the window. Her shoulders stiffened. Fine, if he wanted the list, she'd give it to him. In all its short and sweet beauty. "Robert Wolfe. He was...he was a choreographer that I met years ago."

Brilliant. Determined. Way too exacting.

"Who else."

The impatience in his tone grated. It wasn't like she had a four page list. *I bet he does.* "Evan Meadows, he's an actor." One who'd made it pretty big recently. "But he's in California now so I don't see how he could possibly —"

"Keep going, Skye." His voice was clipped.

There wasn't very far that she *could* go. "Mitch Loxley."

The car's interior got very, very quiet.

"Say the name again," Trace growled.

"Why? You heard me the first time." She glanced out the window once more. A frown pulled her brows low. This definitely wasn't the way to the penthouse.

"You slept with your doctor?" Trace demanded. His voice was low and cold.

Sometimes, he did that. When he was angry, his voice would drop to that lethal softness.

"He wasn't my doctor at the time." She'd been so alone, and Mitch had been the only one there for her. Always smiling. Coming by with doughnuts and flowers.

One night, drinks had led to something...more.

"Why aren't you with him now?"

"Because I couldn't stay in New York." Her lease had been up, and she hadn't had the cash to renew it, not after all her medical bills. Insurance had only stretched so far.

"The *fucking* doctor..."

Her head snapped toward him. "Look, who I've been with shouldn't matter —"

"It matters to me." Gritted. "It matters a great deal."

She would never figure him out. "You've been screwing your way through every model or actress you could find, so don't act like some ex-lover I had does something to you. We both know I made your ancient history list a long time ago."

He leaned toward her. In the darkened interior of the vehicle, she wished that she could see his expression. But he was still hidden by shadows. "It does something," he said. "It makes me fucking furious."

"Trace?"

His hand slid over her cheek. "I want you to forget them. I want to take you to bed, and I want to wipe away every memory you have of them all."

She couldn't take a deep enough breath. "We're over, Trace. You know—"

"How can we be over, when I still want you so much?" His hand slid down her cheek, down her jaw, then down to the column of her throat. His fingers splayed over her neck, lightly touching the pulse that raced frantically beneath her skin. "And how can we be over, when you still want me so much?"

Because he'd ruined her for other men. It was a sad and humiliating fact. The sex had been good with the others, but with Trace...

I was always comparing. How had that been fair? Maybe that was why Robert and Evan had ended things. They'd told her—both of them—that she wouldn't let them get close. That she put up a wall to keep them out of her life.

After Trace, she'd needed that wall. Because she hadn't ever wanted to hurt that much again.

When he left me, I felt broken. It had taken too long for her to put the pieces of her life back together.

"If I'm wrong, tell me now." Trace's hand seemed to singe her skin. "Tell me to back the hell off, and I will. I won't push for something you're not willing to give. I want all of you. All or nothing."

Wasn't that the way it had worked between them before? She *had* given everything to him.

What had Trace given?

The car stopped.

"All or nothing, Skye. Make the choice."

Then he pulled away from her. Shoved open his door.

She sucked in some much needed air. A frantic glance to the left made her realize — *definitely not the penthouse.*

Her door opened. Only Reese wasn't standing there, holding said door. Trace was.

She scrambled out. "What are we doing here?"

And here was — the airport?

"Taking a flight. My jet's waiting."

He had a jet? Right, of course, the mega-wealthy guy he'd become would have his own jet.

Skye didn't step away from the car. "Where are we going?" Why was this like pulling teeth with him? "I have my studio opening, I can't just—"

"You want this SOB caught, don't you? Well, to do that, we need to head back to the beginning. If he started following you in New York, then we can try to learn more about him there."

He seriously thought she was just going to jump on a flight to New York? Right then? "I'm not going to—"

"You can make the people in that city talk to me. The dancers, your old neighbors. By you being with me, they'll share more. Maybe someone saw something. Maybe someone saw *him.*" His fingers still gripped the door. "I need you to come with me. We'll be back before the studio opens, I promise you that."

Once upon a time, she'd loved New York.

But she'd run from it, so desperate to get away.

Only…now she wondered…had she been running from the city? Or from the man who'd been after her? The dark shadow that seemed to stalk her, with every step she took?

Before the accident, she'd started to become so nervous. Jumping at the slightest noise. She hadn't been able to shake the feeling that her actions were being monitored. Watched. *Always watched.*

And he'd been in her home. She knew he had broken inside, even though there had been no indication of a forced entry.

"Let's end this," Trace urged her. "Come with me to New York. Let me do the job that I know how to do. I'll find him, and I *will* stop him."

She glanced toward the waiting airport. A plane had just taken off, and the rumble of its engines filled the air. "All right. I'll come with you."

Reese slammed the trunk. Her head jerked toward him, and she saw that he was carrying two bags. One bag had to belong to Trace, but the other bag—

It's mine.

"I thought you might see things my way," Trace murmured.

Confident, cocky bastard.

He took her hand. "Not still afraid to fly, are you?"

Yes, she was. Terrified.

But she wasn't about to admit that fact to him. He already thought she feared too many things in this world.

I do.

She'd first started to fear when she was eight years old. When her parents hadn't come home from their dinner. When she'd heard her babysitter whispering about an accident. When she'd stood in a graveyard and watched as flowers were put on two caskets.

She'd feared when she went to the first foster home. When she'd gone to the second. To the third.

She'd feared when hard hands had reached for her during the night. When she was hurt. Pain that came again and again. Her only escape had been to dance.

A social worker had introduced Skye to dancing. She'd taken her to a community center, and Skye had gotten lost in the music, in the dance.

She'd danced. Day after day after day.

And she'd feared…

Until she'd looked up and into a pair of bright, angry blue eyes.

The fear had stopped then, for a time.

But it had come back all too soon.

It always returned, eventually.

***

Alex Griffin watched as the private plane taxied down the runway. Jet-setting away…that seemed to fit with the image that was developing for Trace Weston.

He'd been digging into the man's background for most of the day. A kid who'd grown up poor, Weston had entered the Army at twenty. His past had been easy enough to discover up until that point, but after he'd enlisted with Uncle Sam, Trace Weston's records had vanished. There was a four-year hole in the man's past. Four years of seemingly *nothing*.

Then Weston had appeared again in Chicago. He'd appeared and suddenly had deep ties with foreign dignitaries, government agencies. His security company had skyrocketed to the top of the field.

Weston had become a millionaire. No, a billionaire, according to his tax reports.

So why was a guy like that taking such a personal interest in a stalking case? That wasn't even the type of security Weston handled. He worked with corporations, not individuals.

Alex pulled his hands from the pockets of his jacket. He'd already used his badge to gain entrance to the back area of the airport, and he was about to use the shield to help him again. People always talked freely when a badge was involved.

His eyes narrowed as he saw a man rushing away from the runway. "Uh, excuse me, sir..." Alex called out.

The man, older, balding, frowned at him. He wore one of the light blue uniforms typical of the ground crew.

"Were you just working on Trace Weston's plane?" Alex asked, as he kept his badge out.

The fellow glanced at the badge, then back at Alex's face. "Mr. Weston doesn't have any trouble with me. I do my job, I—"

"I never said you didn't," Alex soothed. "I was just curious..."

And he had been curious. He'd pulled up at Skye's studio just in time to see her climb into Weston's car. So he'd followed them, and he'd watched them fly right out of the city.

Strange. An attack one day. A vacation the next?

"Where was Mr. Weston heading?" Alex asked as he cocked his head.

The guy glanced over his shoulder. "I-I think he was going to New York again."

Where Skye Sullivan had lived for so long. "Does he go to New York often?" He could, for business, or for—

"Yeah, he goes there a lot. At least once each week." The man tried to brush by him.

Alex just shifted and blocked his path. "Guys on the ground can sometimes hear stories." And pick up a lot of gossip. "You hear any stories about why Weston visited New York? In the past? Tonight?"

The man smiled, revealing a crooked front tooth. "I don't care why he flies. It just matters that he does. Gives me a job."

Right. This info wasn't helping him.

The guy walked away. Alex glanced up at the sky. Light raindrops were still falling down. He couldn't see the plane any longer.

Maybe Weston had been taking all those trips to the Big Apple strictly for business.

Or maybe...maybe he'd been heading to New York for another reason.

Alex had pulled Skye's accident report. He'd read her statement about someone following her. Forcing her off the road.

The more he probed, the more he worried.

Skye Sullivan was in danger. He just hoped she wasn't putting her trust in the wrong person.

A mistake like that could prove fatal for her.

***

Trace kept his hand curved around Skye as they headed through the hotel's lobby. The marble floor gleamed up at him as the concierge quickly escorted them to the private elevator.

Skye wasn't speaking. She was barely making eye contact with him, and he hated that.

He missed how they used to be.

I'll have that again.

He'd have everything again.

The elevator doors closed, and the ascent began. The elevator slid up, higher and higher.

"Uh, Mr. Weston?" The concierge—Max—cleared his throat. "Is there anything that you'll be needing tonight?"

Trace didn't even try to take his eyes off Skye. She'd slept on the plane. He'd been too wired to even consider dozing off. "I have everything I need." His voice rumbled.

Skye's gaze cut to his.

The elevator's doors opened.

Max scrambled outside. "Y-your suite is waiting, sir. Of course, it's our plaza suite, just as you always request when you visit to see the—"

"I know the suite," Trace cut through his words before Max could say anymore. The fellow was damn chatty tonight.

Max hurriedly opened the suite room door. Skye strode inside. Her head tilted back as she looked up at the massive chandelier that waited in the great room.

"You…um…are you sure you don't want the personal chef to come up?" Max lingered near the door as the bellhop brought in their luggage. "It's late, but never too late for you, Mr. Weston—"

He knew that the personal chef came with the suite. Trace just didn't want the guy up there at that moment. He wanted to be alone with Skye. "Send him up for breakfast," Trace said. His gaze narrowed on the bellhop. "All the bags go in the master bedroom."

Skye had paused at the windows that overlooked Fifth Avenue. It seemed her shoulders tensed.

She'd heard his order about the bags.

But she wasn't arguing.

Yet.

The bellhop and the concierge left a few minutes later. The door eased shut behind them.

Skye kept staring down at the city below. "Sometimes, I forget what New York is like…"

Snow fell lightly past the window. They'd flown out of rain in Chicago and right into a late snowfall in New York.

Her hand lifted and touched the pane of glass. "When I was a kid, New York was everything to me. The people here...they were happy. Famous. Everyone loved them."

When she'd been a kid, she'd bounced from foster home to foster home.

She'd found dancing thanks to a social worker who'd wanted her to have an outlet. That outlet had been at a small, community center. Skye had once told him how nervous she'd been the first day she walked into that center.

She'd been nervous, until she danced.

Skye turned away from the window. "The suite, Trace?" She cleared her throat. "There are only two of us. Do you really think we need...what is this?" She glanced around with pursed lips. "I'm guessing...four thousand square feet?"

"Forty-five hundred." He pulled off his coat. Tossed it aside. Went to her.

"Any room would have worked. Any—"

His hand cupped her chin. "When I was a kid, I dreamed of not being hungry." She would know this. Far better than anyone else. "I dreamed of not wearing someone else's used clothes. Of not being the one mocked because my shoes had holes in them." His parents hadn't died like Skye's. His parents just hadn't given a shit.

They'd forgotten him most days. Left him to feed and clothe himself.

The day the social workers had come for him...*how long had I been without food then?*

His old man loved to use his fist. His mother...she loved to use her bottles. She'd drowned out reality and hadn't cared when her son cried.

"I pulled myself out of the past," he told Skye, making sure he kept his hold gentle. With her, he tried for gentleness. Only for her. "These days, I can afford any damn thing I want."

"What you want..."

His fingers drifted down her throat. She had such a sensitive neck. Once upon a time, he'd kissed her there, and she'd melted for him. "What I want is you." Being near her drove him fucking insane. Having her scent—sweet vanilla—wrap around him. Having her silken skin beneath his fingers.

She wasn't telling him no. Wasn't pushing him away. Instead, she stared up at him with need in her green gaze. "I thought...I thought we came here to figure out who was after me." Her words were a whisper.

"We did." But it was nearing 3 a.m. New York might be the city that never slept, but they still couldn't go pounding on doors right then. Better to wait. Head out in the morning.

Waiting left them with the night.

His fingers eased under the heavy curtain of her hair. Her breath caught on a little rasp that was the sexiest sound he'd heard in years.

"Tell me you haven't thought about us." Even though she'd been with others. *Fucking bastards.* When she'd told him their names, everything had gone red for him. Other men, touching *her*. He wanted to wipe the memory of their hands away.

Trace wanted her to only think of him.

Before the night was over, she would.

"I won't lie." The snow fell lightly behind her. "I've thought about you more times than I can count."

Good. Because every damn night when he closed his eyes, she was the one in his dreams.

Her hand rose. Curled around his wrist. "And I think about the way you told me...*to get the hell out of your life.*"

Trace didn't let his expression alter.

"You stopped wanting me, Trace, not the other way around." She yanked his hand away from her. Marched around him. "Since you got the bell hop to leave my bags in the master bedroom, I'll take that room." She wasn't looking back at him. "With forty-five hundred square feet, I'm sure you can find some other place to crash."

Every muscle in his body locked down. "I never stopped." His control seemed razor thin right then, and that was dangerous. He'd intended a seduction for her.

The wild hunger he'd held in check wasn't supposed to break free.

Not yet.

Her laugh was bitter. Not like Skye at all. "Right. That's why you came after me, huh? Why I've seen you pictured with dozens of women over the years? Because you wanted..."She glared over her shoulder, "*me* so much."

Maybe he wasn't the only one eaten by jealousy. Maybe there was some hope for them after all.

"Want me to prove how much I want you?" Nothing could have kept him away from her in that moment. He'd talked to her doctor before he left Chicago. Skye was safe. The concussion wasn't an issue. She could sleep.

She could fuck.

She was most definitely about to get fucked.

Skye rounded on him. "That isn't—"

He kissed her. There was simply no holding back. He'd waited until they were alone. Waited until he had her in the suite with him.

Waited...waited ten long years.

There was no more waiting.

Unless Skye told him no, unless she didn't want him, he would have her.

CHAPTER FOUR

She should push him away. Skye knew her hands should lift and shove against Trace's chest. Those traitorous hands *shouldn't* be lifting and curving around his shoulders.

She needed to push him away.

Not pull him closer.

But she wanted him closer.

She. Wanted. *Him.*

Her emotions were too raw. Maybe it was the city. Maybe it was Trace. Maybe she was just too scared and too tired of being alone.

But when his tongue thrust into her mouth, when she tasted his rich, masculine flavor, Skye stopped thinking about why it was wrong to be with him.

Right then, she wanted to be wrong.

His mouth was strong and fierce on hers. Searching for a response that she was eager to give. Trace was a great kisser, one who'd just gotten better with age. His lips and his tongue played her perfectly.

And his hands…

His hands stroked down her body. His fingers curled around her hips — then he lifted her up.

Skye gasped because she hadn't been expecting that move, even though she knew how strong he was. Her gasp let him deepen the kiss, and he took two steps and pinned her against the wall.

Her legs locked around his hips. His arousal pressed against her core. Long and hard and thick.

Their clothes were in the way.

Skin to skin. She needed to be that way with him. Needed *desperately* to be that way.

Her hips arched toward him.

His mouth pulled from hers. Trace began to kiss his way down her neck. Right there. Yes, yes, right *there.* Where her neck curved into her shoulder. She loved it when he kissed her —

"You won't forget me," his words were growled against her overheated flesh. "But you will forget them."

He was carrying her again. Down the hallway. Another chandelier glittered overhead. They turned, and he took her into the bedroom.

The big bed took up half of the massive space. The curtains were pulled back. The snow was still falling. Beautiful snow, covering the world in a blanket of white.

He lowered her onto the bed.

She thought he'd follow her. That he'd put his body against hers and crush her into the mattress. She wanted wild passion. Wanted to feel the surge of pleasure that would banish her fear and the past.

But he just stared down at her. "You're even more fucking beautiful now."

She couldn't be. She had on old leggings. A sweatshirt. Her hair was a tangle around her head and —

He started with her shoes. Tossed them aside. Tossed aside the leggings and the sweatshirt. Trace stripped her with deft hands, hands that must have undressed plenty of women.

Jealousy bit into her. *Don't go there, don't.*

Soon she was clad only in the slip of her black bra and her matching panties. She was spread on the bed. He still stood above her.

His gaze traveled slowly, so very slowly, over her body. His jaw hardened when his gaze landed on her bra—her breasts. "So perfect."

No, she was too small there, she was—

His bright stare drifted over the plane of her belly. Down to the flare of her hips.

Trace licked his lips.

She imagined him licking her.

But…but his gaze didn't stay. Down, down it went, and some of her passion began to fade.

My leg. I don't want him looking at my leg.

She didn't want Trace to see the tangled mass of scars that still covered her calf. The scars that would *always* cover the skin.

Why hadn't she turned off the lights? She'd turned them off with Mitch, and she should have thought to turn them off with Trace.

"Don't," her voice sharpened as she tried to reach for him.

Trace caught her hands. Pushed them back against the mattress. Fully clothed, he came down on top of her. "Don't what, baby? Don't look at you?" His lips—open, hot, sexy—brushed over hers. "Don't taste? Because that's exactly what I plan to do. I'll taste every inch of you."

Don't pity me. Those were the words she'd meant to say. But he wasn't looking at her calf any longer. He was kissing her and holding her wrists prisoner.

She liked the friction of his clothes against her. Liked the feel of that strong, hard body over hers.

Her legs were parted. His hips pushed against her sex, and it was good. So good.

He'd make it better. She knew he would.

"That's what I'm doing tonight, baby," the words rumbled against her lips. "I'm tasting, and I'm taking…everything."

He lifted her hands above her head. Switched his hold so that just one of his hands imprisoned hers. Then his left hand snaked down her body.

Her bra was tossed across the room.

The cool air hit her nipples, making them go even tighter.

Then his mouth was on her. His mouth wasn't cool. It was hot. Seeming to singe her and the rasp of his tongue against her nipples felt so *good*.

She was wet. She could feel the wetness on her panties, and Skye wanted them gone. She wanted Trace thrusting into her—

"I'll let your hands go, but don't move them. I get to touch. I get to taste." His hands eased away from hers. "I get to take."

She would be taking her pleasure, too. Trace liked to be in control in the bedroom, dominant, compelling and—

He was kissing his way down her body. His dark stubble pressed into her stomach. His tongue licked over her skin.

His fingers slid under the edge of her panties. "Fuck, yes," he muttered. "Wet for me."

She didn't want to wait any longer. "Trace, *now*."

"No." He pulled the panties down her legs. Then his fingers slid up her thighs. Teased. Tormented her. "I've waited too long. I told you, I get to taste and take."

Everything.

Her hands balled into fists so that she wouldn't reach out to him.

It's just sex. It's just sex. The mantra flew through her head as her heart raced. She had to focus on the present, not the past. Everything got so tangled up when she was with him.

This wasn't about love.

Sex. Pleasure.

His fingers slid between her legs. Pushed between the folds of her sex. *Into* her.

She arched off the bed. His thumb rubbed over her clit even as he thrust two fingers into her.

More. "Trace..." Skye could barely gasp out his name.

"You're so gorgeous like this..." His words were dark, deep. "Flushed, open, ready for me...only me."

His hands withdrew. No, dammit, she'd been *close.*

"Say it's only me, Skye."

Her lashes lifted. She didn't even remember closing her eyes.

"Say it." His mouth lowered to her sex. His lips pressed against her, and if his hands hadn't moved to hold her hips against the mattress, she would have leapt off the bed at the first, electric touch of his tongue against her sex.

Pleasure beat at her as he tasted her. Her body twisted against the mattress. She wasn't trying to get away from him. Skye wanted to get closer. Her fingers splayed wide, then grabbed the thick covers, bunching them in her fists.

Release was near, so near—

"Tell me, Skye," he demanded. A dark note had entered his voice. One that should have made her hesitate. Possessive... fierce... "Only me."

She hovered on the brink of release. "Trace, I need more—"

"I'll give you every fucking thing."

A zipper hissed down. He lowered his body against hers. He thrust into her.

Not easy. Not tentative.

He drove deep, filling her completely, and she stopped being on the brink. Pleasure flooded through her. She gasped as her heart raced, seeming to pound right out of her chest. Her whole body tightened as that release swept over her. So good...so perfect...on and on and on.

Trace kept thrusting. He grabbed her legs. Lifted them higher. Made her take more and more until she was frantic because another release was coming. She was hollowed out from the first one, but he was pushing the second wave on her, and she screamed this time, a broken yell because the pleasure hit her so hard.

Then he came. A hard, hot jet inside of her. "Only..." he growled.

She didn't hear the rest of what he said. Her racing heartbeat drowned out the words, but she knew.

Only me.

Trace shuddered against her. He'd come, she'd felt that release, but he kept thrusting.

The pleasure didn't end.

She'd never felt this way with anyone else. Never wanted and wanted and had her whole body explode with pleasure, one shattering climax after the other.

No one else.

Only Trace.

She hadn't given him the words. But then, she didn't need to.

He already knew.

Only me.

***

Rehearsal was always a chaotic time. Dancers swirled around the stage. Choreographers jumped in, corrected, advised. The director was there, shouting orders in the background.

It seemed both incredibly familiar and oddly foreign as Skye stood in the shadows, watching everyone else. It was barely past seven a.m., but, of course the dancers were working. By this time, they would have been working for at least two hours.

Sweating. Flying. Dancing until their muscles trembled.

This had been her life.

Without it, she'd been lost.

"Skye?" She recognized that voice, with its faint English accent. She'd known that Robert Wolfe would be there — since he was the lead choreographer, he had to be there. And Trace had been determined to question Robert. But...

Robert isn't doing this to me.

She didn't want to suspect him.

She turned at his call, her shoulder brushing against Trace's. They hadn't spoken much that morning. She'd felt too raw, too overexposed after last night.

Just how fast did you tumble into bed with him? The question whispered through her mind. The answer? *Fast. Very. Very fast.*

A broad smile split Robert's handsome face as he hurried toward her. He was sweating, the shine gleaming on him, because he'd been working with the dancers. He rushed toward her and wrapped her in a tight hug, sweat and all.

"I knew you'd come back," Robert said as he squeezed her even tighter. "You just needed time. You just — "

"I-I'm not here to dance."

He stopped squeezing her. Robert pulled back, but didn't release her. He stared down at her, a faint line between his perfect brows.

Robert was tall, with a strong dancer's body. His blond hair was brushed away from the strong planes of his face, and his tanned skin gleamed under the lights.

"You can let her go now," Trace ordered him. But then Trace didn't wait for Robert to comply. He pulled the other man away from Skye.

"Jeez, Skye, picked a jealous lover, eh?"

She could feel the blush on her cheeks. Skye cleared her throat. "We...we need to talk. Somewhere private."

Robert's face hardened. "Something's wrong."

Something had been wrong, for a very long time.

"The dressing rooms." He motioned toward the right. "While everyone's rehearsing, they're empty."

She knew the way, so Skye started walking first. She'd only taken a few steps when she realized exactly what Robert was doing.

He was watching her walk. No, more specifically, he was watching her leg. Dammit, had she limped? She didn't want to limp in front of him. She didn't like to limp in front of anyone. But especially Robert. He'd trained her for so long. Told her that she was the best dancer he'd ever seen.

Oh, how the mighty had fallen.

Skye straightened her shoulders. Slowed her stride.

A few moments later, they were in her old dressing room. Memories were everywhere in that room. She'd been so excited when she came in after a performance. So—

"You look...familiar to me," Robert said as he closed the door and let his gaze focus on Trace.

"He's Trace Weston," Skye said, waving her hand toward him. "You've probably seen his picture in the paper."

Robert gave a little whistle. "Right. I have seen you." The whistle was more mocking than anything else. Robert didn't look impressed. But then, if you weren't talking about dancing, Robert normally *wasn't* impressed.

His golden gaze turned back to her. "I want you to dance for me again."

Skye tensed. She'd been afraid that he'd go right back to that.

Before she could reply, Trace put his body between them. "Have you been to Chicago recently, Wolfe?"

"Chicago? No, no, of course not." His British accent tightened the words. "I've been here, for the last bloody month. Trying to make those dancers out there *half* as good as Skye..." He stepped around Trace. Smiled at Skye. "Have you ever seen her dance?" Robert asked Trace. His eyes didn't leave Skye's face. "It's the most fucking beautiful thing in the world."

"I've seen her," Trace's voice was clipped.

Trace had seen her long ago. In a different lifetime. When he'd taken her to the community center. Stayed to watch her practice. She'd gotten much better than the way she'd been then.

Well, she *had* been better.

"We're not here about the dancing," she tried telling Robert again. The man had such a one track mind. "There's something else that we need to discuss."

"Something more important than you getting that sweet ass of yours back onstage? Doubt it. I don't see you—"

"Someone is stalking, Skye." Trace's cold, quiet words cut right through the rumble of Robert's speech. "Some bastard attacked her recently in Chicago."

"Skye!" Robert's jaw dropped. "Why didn't you call me? Why didn't you—"

"She said that the man first started following her here in New York. He got into her dressing room..." Trace cast an angry glance around the room. "Since the security here is non-existent, I can see how that happened. He got into this place, he got into her home, and—"

"And you said someone forced you off the road," Robert muttered. He ran a shaking hand over his face. "Hell, I thought it was the pain meds talking. When you first woke up, you were out of it in that hospital. I didn't realize..." His words trailed off.

Maybe because he'd just fully noticed the killing glare that Trace had aimed on him.

"You think it's me, mate?" Robert demanded, backing up a step.

"You sure have easy access to her dressing room, *mate*," Trace threw right back. "You know where she lived."

"Of course, I did! I helped her move in! Dammit, I even had her back-up key."

Trace's shoulders stiffened. He turned and cast that rather scary glare of his at Skye.

Crap. Had she neglected to mention that part?

"But I wouldn't do that to Skye! I would *never* do anything to hurt her." And Robert reached for Skye again. His fingers locked around her arms. "You know how much I need you. I wouldn't hurt you, not for—"

"Get your fucking hands off her."

Goosebumps rose on Skye's skin.

Robert immediately jerked away from her. "Look, mate, I—"

Trace caught Skye's hand and pulled her to his side. "I'm going to need confirmation that you haven't left the city."

"Y-you're asking me for an alibi?" Robert sputtered.

"Damn straight, I am."

Now Robert was the one to flush. "A dozen dancers can tell you that I've been working their asses off for the last twenty days. They can all confirm that I haven't left the city."

"Good." Trace flashed a hard smile, one that held an evil edge. "I'll get them to confirm that before I leave today."

Skye's breath expelled in a fast rush. "Robert, did you ever see anyone hanging around my dressing room? Anyone that lingered after a show?" She'd asked stagehands the same questions before, but no one had seen anything. After a performance, it was too chaotic to keep track of people.

Robert's eyes had narrowed on Trace. He seemed to be searching Trace's face with a dark intensity.

"Robert?" Skye pushed.

"There are always fans who try to get back to the dancers," Robert said, rolling his shoulders. "I've told you before, when you dance, you become something...quite different."

That...different...had been what drew him to her. A night of long practice had turned into something more for them. But it hadn't lasted with Robert. It never lasted because...

No other man is Trace.

"You didn't see anyone?" Trace questioned. "Dammit, what about video cameras?"

"We don't have them backstage." Robert shook his head. "After a show, it's chaos. Plain and simple. Hell, do you have any idea just how many flowers get delivered after a show? It's a fuckin' madhouse here."

And someone had slipped into that madhouse far too easily.

"I'll check, okay?" Robert offered as a knock sounded at the door. "I'll ask around and see if anyone remembers anything but, Skye, you know how fast the back-stage groups turn over. We've got new staff working this show."

With every new show, there was a rotation.

A knock rapped again at the door. "Wolfe!" A woman's voice called. "They need you on stage."

"Be right there." He straightened his shoulders. Met Trace's stare. "Check my alibi. Talk to the dancers. Like I said, I would *never* hurt Skye, and I sure hope you find the bastard who did." Then he glanced her way. The gold in his eyes heated. "Come back to me. I want you to dance for me again."

Angry tension seemed to roll off Trace's body.

"I...can't," Skye said softly.

"How do you know?" Robert asked her, tilting his head as he studied her. "Unless you try?"

The knock pounded again. It was much more impatient this time. "Wolfe, they're screwing up out here! We need you."

He gave a curt nod to Skye and Trace, and Robert hurried away.

The door hung open behind him, just a few inches.

"Before we leave," Trace spoke slowly, "*I'll* talk to the stagehands here and see if anyone remembers something."

She nodded. "It's been too long, hasn't it?" If Trace had been here to question people sooner, to run his investigation, then perhaps more evidence, more clues could have been found.

Trace exhaled slowly. "I'll find him. He's not getting away."

She hoped that he wasn't. She started to slip by Trace.

He caught her arm. "You left New York without trying to dance again? You just ran from the city?"

Her throat had gone dry. "It took me weeks to walk again." That was only *after* all of the surgeries. "And I did try." That painful memory would never go away. "The first time I tried to dance, I fell on my face." The first time, the second, the third. Her lashes lifted so that she could meet that bright blue stare. "Robert is the most demanding choreographer I've ever worked with. I knew what he would see if he watched me dance. I didn't want to hear him say—"

You've lost it, love.

She could hear his words clearly in her mind.

"There are some things that you know on your own." She'd had enough humiliation and pain by that point. Running had seemed like her best plan. *Escape.*

And she didn't want to talk about this anymore. "I'll go talk to some of the dancers." Her words tumbled out quickly. "I'll see if anyone remembers or—or maybe if anyone had something like this happen to them." So she was grasping at straws. That room was too small. Too filled with memories, and Skye wanted to get *out* of there.

So she fled. After all, she might suck at walking sometimes, but when it came to running away, she had that one down cold.

***

The Brit was a bastard who touched Skye far too freely. Trace could still feel the jealousy coursing through him.

You came back to me.

The hell she had. Skye hadn't turned to Wolfe when she needed protection.

She'd gone to Trace.

The dancers and the stagehands had been no help. They didn't remember anything.

Or anyone.

Plenty of fans had come to see Skye, but their faces were a blur in everyone's memories.

Useless.

So they'd left the dancers and the choreographer who watched Skye with far too much intensity. They'd moved to the second stop on their list.

He'd visited this place before. So many times, when Skye hadn't even known he was there. *I had to make sure she was all right.*

"It's been a while," Skye murmured beside him as they strode down the hospital corridor. "And I can't exactly say I'm happy to be back here."

The scent of disinfectant filled his nose. Nurses bustled past him. A family walked down the corridor, carrying flowers and balloons in their hands.

Skye's doctor was on duty that day. Trace had verified Dr. Mitch Loxley's rotation schedule before heading to the hospital. He'd also had his men check to see if either Mitch

Loxley or Robert Wolfe had taken any recent flights to Chicago.

They hadn't.

But they could have driven over there. A thirteen-hour drive was doable.

He halted at the nurse's station. "I need to see Dr. Loxley."

The nurse glanced up. Her eyes widened a bit as she stared at Trace, then she smiled.

He'd gotten plenty of smiles like hers over the years. Flirtatious. Interested.

Only he wasn't interested. Skye was at his side.

When he had her, he didn't need anyone else.

"He's on his rounds right now, but is there something I can help you with?" The nurse asked as she rose — and leaned forward, putting her hand on his arm. "I'll be happy to help you, if you need assistance."

What he needed was Loxley.

Another of Skye's lovers.

Shit, but it had been hard not to drive his fist into Wolfe's pretty-boy face. When the guy kept touching Skye, too much familiarity in that touch...*I wanted to break his hand.*

Only Trace wasn't supposed to be that guy any longer. He was supposed to be the businessman. The success story.

Not the street fighter who wanted to tear into anyone who'd gotten too close to Skye.

"I'm afraid that only Dr. Loxley can help *us,*" he said, pulling Skye close to his side. She'd tensed up when they walked into the hospital. Not that he blamed her, not after what she'd been through. He wanted to question the doctor, then get the hell out of that place with her.

He'd prefer to get her back to the hotel. To get her naked in his bed again.

Once wasn't nearly enough.

But he had to eliminate the threats around her first.

"When are you expecting Loxley back?" Trace asked the blonde nurse.

Then, speak of the damn devil, Loxley marched around the corner. The guy's white lab coat swirled around him as he put a clipboard on the nurse's station. "Marsha, make sure the low carb diet for Mr. Rodriguez continues for at least twenty-four more hours and..." He trailed off.

Because his gaze had lifted.

And locked on Skye.

Another asshole that I want to punch.

But, at least unlike Robert, Loxley didn't rush across the room and wrap Skye in a too-tight hug.

Loxley didn't move at all, but his gaze sure seemed to drink Skye in.

What was it about her? She drew men to her. She'd sure drawn him easily enough.

Addicted him, from the very first.

"Dr. Loxley." With an effort, Trace kept all the emotion from his voice. "We need a few minutes of your time."

The guy's startled gaze flew to his. The doc hadn't even seemed aware of the fact that Trace was standing there, not until that moment.

Trace wasn't used to being ignored.

He flashed his teeth in a shark's grin. "We're going to need that time, now."

"I-I just finished my rounds." Loxley glanced at his watch. "I can spare a few minutes. Come this way." Then he turned, without another word, and headed back down the corridor.

Trace took his time following the doc, and he made sure not to let go of Skye.

How did she feel about the doctor? The fellow was close to Trace's height, had a build similar to Trace...Mitch Loxley even had the same dark hair.

Mitch Loxley seemed like a safer, more dependable version of Trace.

Trace hated the sonofabitch.

Files were scattered around the doctor's office. A few framed photographs. The doc grabbed the files and shoved them on his desk, blocking some of those photos.

But Trace had already seen them.

Yes, he *hated* the SOB.

"What are you doing here, Skye?" Loxley asked as he crossed his arms over his chest. Now that they were away from the nurse's station, the polite veneer that the doc had worn while they had an audience showed signs of cracking. "I thought you'd gone to Chicago."

He knew where she'd headed.

"I did." Skye pulled her hand from Trace's. "Do you...do you remember when I said that someone forced me off the road?"

Mitch's dark eyebrows shot up. "*That's* why you're here? The cops told you that there were no signs of—"

"Someone attacked me recently, in Chicago." Her voice was soft. "Before the attack, someone had been following me for days, weeks...the same way the person followed me here, in New York."

The faint lines near Mitch's eyes deepened. "Look, you were under a lot of stress after the accident, I get that...but the cops said—"

"I'm not real interested in what the cops said," Trace cut in. He wasn't in the mood to have this pompous prick dismiss Skye's fears. "I'm interested in what Skye says. Someone attacked her, and I'm here to find out who that was."

Loxley's brown eyes darted from Skye to Trace. "Are you some kind of bodyguard or something?"

"Something."

Those brown eyes assessed Trace. "I've seen you before." Mitch's fingers snapped together. "You were at the hospital, back when Skye was first brought in. The admins upstairs forced us to let you in to see her."

With the right leverage, he'd found his way to Skye's bedside. The fact that he'd made a hefty donation to the hospital's charity board had certainly helped his situation.

Mitch's eyes widened. "You're Trace Weston."

Trace shrugged.

"Trace," the doctor gritted as his gaze jumped to Skye. "I've heard that name before, haven't I?"

She flinched.

What the hell is that about?

"I should have known," Loxley continued, "when you told me you were headed back to Chicago, that you'd wind up with him." He exhaled. "I don't know what you want from me, Skye. You left and—*hold the hell up.*" A muscle flexed in his jaw as the doc seemed to fully grasp the situation. "You think it was me? You think I'm the one who came after you?"

"Are you?" Trace asked him.

The color had fled from Skye's face. Trace didn't like that. Not at all.

"I didn't even *know* her before the accident. So I sure couldn't have been stalking her then." Mitch threw himself into his chair. The wheels rolled back. "And, no, I didn't rush after her to Chicago. The sex was good, but trust me, I've moved the hell on."

The sex was good. Every muscle in Trace's body tensed.

"Give us a moment, would you, Skye?" Trace's voice was soft. Too soft.

"Trace..." Worry had entered her voice. She did still know him so well.

He glanced at her. "It will only take a moment."

Skye shook her head. "I'm not going anywhere. This is *my* life we're talking about."

The drumming of his heartbeat filled Trace's ears. He forced himself to look back at the doctor. "Do you remember who visited Skye while she was here?"

"I remember you," Loxley snapped. "I don't forget it when the hospital VP tells me I have to let some visitor in against regulations."

The guy needed to stop pushing. "Anyone else?"

"I have a lot of patients, it's not like I can remember everything—"

"You don't fuck all your patients." Trace paused. "At least, I hope you don't. So since Skye warranted *special* treatment from you, I'm thinking you might have paid a bit more attention to who was coming and going from her room."

The doctor's eyes had narrowed. Anger burned in his dark gaze. "The British guy," Mitch bit out. "Wolfe. He came in, so did some of the women she danced with. I never saw anyone else, but then, I was working my rounds. Treating other patients. Not keeping a twenty-four seven watch on Skye."

The doctor just kept pushing…

"I guess I know why you told me good-bye, Skye," Loxley said as he drummed his fingers on the desk. "But then, I knew what was happening after that night."

"I'm sorry," Skye told him.

Trace stiffened. Oh, hell, no, she didn't need to apologize to this jerk who didn't understand the whole concept of a doctor-patient relationship.

"So am I," Loxley murmured. His gaze shifted to the door. Jaw hard, he said, "Now if that's all, I have work to do."

No, that wasn't all. "I need to know where you've been the last few days, doctor." Though Trace had a feeling that friendly nurse Marsha could give him that info.

"Why? Because you think I flew to Chicago and attacked Skye?" Mitch rose from his chair. Crossed the small room until he stood right in front of Skye. "Is that what you think? That I would hurt you? I'm the one who saved your life. I'm the one who helped you."

"It's not like that, Mitch," Skye said. There was some bite in her voice. "I'm just trying to figure out what's happening. You don't understand—he's been watching me. For so long." Her hair slid over her shoulders as she shook her head. "I'm tired of being afraid. I want him stopped. I thought...*we* thought you might have seen someone, seen something that could help—"

"If I knew anything that would help you, I'd tell you." Mitch's gaze swept over her face. "I'm sorry, but I don't."

Skye nodded. She turned away. Trace headed to her side. He took her elbow.

Made sure that she exited that room.

But...before he left...

Trace shut the door. He flipped the lock so that Skye couldn't burst back inside. Then he squared off against the doctor.

"I don't really care for bullshit." Trace figured it was good to be blunt.

Skye knocked on the door. "Trace?" Her voice was high, shocked. "What the hell are you doing?"

He pointed to the desk. "If you're so over Skye, why is her picture on your desk?"

The doc's Adam's apple bobbed.

"You better have people here who can say that you haven't left town. Because if I find out that you've been following Skye..." Trace smiled and knew the sight would chill. "I will make sure that you're never a threat to her again."

"I-I didn't even realize the photo was still there. I just haven't tossed it out—"

"You're done with Skye. She's done with you. She's moved the fuck on, and you need to do the same." Trace held the guy's gaze a moment longer, wanting to make sure the fellow got the point.

Skye's fist hit the door. "Trace, *stop it!*" Fear and anger twined in that demand.

Because she remembered what he was like. She shouldn't worry so much. He was leaving the doctor in one piece. For the moment.

The sex was good.

"It might have just been good with you," Trace said as he cast a disdainful glance at the doc. "But it's fucking fantastic with me."

Then he left the not-so-good doctor glaring after him.

"What did you do?" Skye pounced on him.

He shrugged. "Set a few things straight."

Now it was time to find that nurse and confirm Mitch Loxley's whereabouts.

The door slammed closed behind him. Trace was pretty sure he heard a fist hit the wood.

Good. The message had been received.

***

She belonged with him.

Skye had to see it. No one else would do for her. No one else could match her the way he did.

They were meant to be.

Her sweet scent still filled his lungs. Her face haunted his nights.

He couldn't get away from her.

He'd make sure she didn't escape from him.

There was no place that she could hide. He'd been watching her for too long. He knew all her secrets.

Beautiful Skye carried so many secrets.

She wasn't the good girl that people thought her to be. Wasn't the sweet sleeping beauty in need of true love's kiss.

Skye had a dark side. That was why he was so drawn to her.

Skye's darkness matched his own.

No one would come between them.

Not now.

Not ever.

He'd see Skye dead first.

CHAPTER FIVE

"The trip was a waste of time." The plane flew through the air, the sound of its engines not even penetrating the lush interior. Skye's fingers fumbled with the clasp of her seatbelt.

Trace sat across from her. His legs were spread, brushing against hers, and a glass of whiskey was held loosely in his hand.

"I told you before…none of those men would do this." Her ex's. Since Evan was shooting a film in Hawaii, he'd been ruled off Trace's suspect list. At least, she hoped that he had.

Both Mitch and Robert's alibis had checked out. Four dancers had backed up Robert. And the nurse with the too-big breasts had been quick to fill in Trace about Mitch's recent activities.

"I needed to see them," Trace took a long drink of the whiskey, "and their reaction to you."

"To me? Uh, they didn't exactly have a reaction—"

He downed the rest of the whiskey in a fast gulp. "Robert views you as a possession. *His* possession. A dancer that he controls."

Yes, he did. She glanced out the darkened window. That was the reason she'd broken things off with him. Not that there had been much to break-off. They'd only been together a week when she realized she'd made a serious mistake by getting intimately involved with him.

"As for the doctor, he was lying through his teeth." Trace sat the empty glass down beside him.

"What do you mean?" Marsha had said that Mitch hadn't left town in over two months. Trace had seemed doubtful, but Marsha had pulled out appointment calendars that were filled with patient listings—all tying back to Mitch.

"Mitch Loxley would take you back in an instant if he could. He probably still jerks off to you at night."

Her mouth dropped open. He had *not* just said that to her. "You can't know that..."

"Sure I can. Because I did the same damn thing until I got you back." Trace unhooked his seatbelt. Stared at her with glittering eyes. "Come here, Skye."

She didn't want to move. "We didn't learn anything useful in New York." Why had her voice gone all husky?

His hot gaze stayed on hers. "I got a chance to talk personally with the cops. I went over the police report for your accident. I actually learned a hell of a lot."

She shook her head. "We don't know who's doing this—"

"Come here."

His voice had deepened.

"I'm right here." Her heart was pounding too hard and fast in her chest. She shifted her legs restlessly. Brushed them against his. The move hadn't been deliberate, had it?

"That's not close enough." His fingers tapped against the armrests on either side of his seat. "I like that skirt on you."

It wasn't like she'd had a lot of clothing choices. Since he'd been the one to pack for this little trip, she'd had to take what she could get.

Right then, Skye wore a long, black skirt and matching top. Underneath that skirt?

Thigh highs. Her garter belt.

"What did the doctor mean when he said, '*after that night*'?"

Her breath burned in her lungs. She did not want to make this confession. She needed to keep a little pride.

"Skye..."

Her head jerked. "It doesn't matter. We're over."

"You and Loxley are." He hadn't moved from his seat. "But you and I are just getting started." His gaze swept over her. "Why are you afraid of me?"

That question caught her off guard. "I'm not!" An instant denial.

"Of course, you are. You've been afraid of me since the night we met."

She didn't want to remember that night. "You saved me then."

"I scared you because I was so violent. Because in that one instant, you saw the real me—the me that I try so hard to hide from everyone else."

The man who'd walked a razor's edge of violence. Who'd attacked with a stunning fury.

"No other woman has seen me like that." His gaze returned to pin hers. "I try to take care with them, to make sure that I hold myself in check."

She couldn't look away from him. "I don't want you to pretend to be someone else with me."

"I don't. Not with you." His right hand lifted. Opened toward her. "And that's why you're scared. Because you know how dangerous I can be, and you still want me."

Yes, she did.

Skye found herself rising. Walking those few feet that separated them and reaching for his offered hand.

He immediately pulled her down on top of him. In seconds, Trace had her positioned so that her legs draped over his. So that her sex pushed down against the firm ridge of his arousal.

His lips were on her neck, kissing her lightly. "Tell me about that night...the night the doctor lost you."

Her eyes squeezed shut.

His fingers slid under the skirt. Trailed lightly up her thigh. Her muscles tightened beneath that touch.

"I don't want to talk about him." She wouldn't.

His fingers pushed a little higher. Her body was tense, aching. If he would just move his fingers up a little bit more...

"What do you want, Skye?"

She forced herself to open her eyes. To meet his bright stare. "I want you." No hesitation. No lies.

His head tilted. "The pilot is close by. What if he hears you?"

Her heart beat a little faster at that. "I-I won't make a sound."

"I've made you scream before."

Her breath sawed from her lungs. His fingers had risen up a few more inches. She felt them at the edge of her panties. Then...then he was touching her through the soft silk. Rubbing over her and she pressed down into his hand. "I won't make a sound," she whispered again.

"We'll see..." Trace murmured. His fingers slipped under the silk. "Oh, baby, you're already wet for me." His fingers caressed her sex, teasing her, tormenting her.

Skye's hands locked on the seat behind his head. She squeezed tightly when his index finger thrust into her.

That wasn't enough. She needed more from him.

His thumb pressed over the center of her clit. Pressed, rotated, and had her hips thrusting desperately against his hand.

Her nails sank into that seat when a second finger pushed into her.

He kissed her neck. His tongue licked her skin, then she felt the faint bite of his teeth. "You want to come, don't you?"

She was almost—

"But not yet," he said, and his fingers eased back. Stroked, but didn't push her toward that wild rush for pleasure. "Not just yet."

Her head turned. Their eyes met.

"Tell me about that night."

What the hell?

She shoved away from the seat, away from *him*. "No." Why did he have to know everything about her? Some shames were her own.

Skye tried to scramble back into her seat. Forget being graceful. She would just fall on her ass if necessary. Whatever. Anything to escape.

But he didn't let her go. He pulled her back against him, and the long, thick bulge of his arousal pressed into her damp panties. "There's nowhere to run."

Not when they were nearly thirty thousand feet up in the air.

"And you don't want to run, not from me. I'm the one you ran to." His mouth was on her neck again. On that spot where her shoulder and neck met. On the spot that always made her weak.

She hated being so weak with him. So vulnerable. He shouldn't have such power over her body. Over her. He shouldn't—

He's not the only one with power.

Determination filled her. She wasn't going to play his game. She'd show Trace that his need for her blazed just as hot as her own.

Her hands pushed between them. Found that heavy length of arousal. She stroked him through the pants that he wore. His cock jerked beneath her touch.

"*Skye...*"

"The plane will land soon. I'm done talking." She'd been through enough. She unbuttoned his fly. Unzipped his pants. No underwear. Typical for Trace. Her fingers closed around him, and she pumped his flesh. Once, twice.

Touching him turned her on. That was her weakness.

It was his, too.

His breath hissed out. His fingers pushed into her sex again, thrusting hard and deep even as she pumped him. It was good, so good, hands stroking, caressing. She still had her skirt on. Her bra, her panties...he'd just shoved those panties to the side.

He was hot and hard and strong in her hand. Moisture gleamed on the head of his arousal, and she knew that just a few more—

"Not that way," he snarled, the words dark and hard. "*In* you."

Her panties ripped. He lifted her hips. Her skirt swirled around them. He lifted her—and thrust deep.

He filled her completely with that one thrust. So full that she couldn't move for an instant. Her knees were on either side of his hips. One of her knees jammed into the armrest— she didn't *care*.

Trace started to move again. No, he moved her. Lifting her up, bringing her crashing back down.

"Can you...stay quiet...?" He rasped the words as the black of his pupils spread in his eyes. "Or will you scream...for me?"

Her heart raced faster, seeming to jump from her chest. His hand was still stroking the center of her need, and he had her angled so that every thrust sent his cock over her most sensitive flesh.

His open pants brushed against her legs. *Still dressed. We're both—*

"I like it when you scream."

Her release was coming. Tightening her body. Spiraling up and blazing through her.

He thrust harder. Harder. His grip was so tight, she wondered if it might bruise her.

Then she—

Trace drove deep.

She exploded with a release so hard and consuming that her whole body shuddered. A cry broke from her lips.

"Yes, hell, *yes.*" Trace found his own pleasure. A hot tide filled her as he came.

For a few moments, she couldn't see anything. She could only feel the pleasure that shook her body in hard, desperate waves. Her breath wasn't deep enough. Her heart couldn't slow down.

"So fucking beautiful..." He brushed back her hair. Kissed her.

Was that the first time he'd kissed her on that plane?

She blinked, and some of the darkness seemed to fade.

"We're about to begin our descent..." The pilot's voice floated to her. "Please make sure you're buckled."

Heat burned her face.

Trace just laughed.

She'd screamed. Right at the end there, she'd screamed for him.

Fumbling, Skye pulled away from Trace. Her panties were on the floor. She grabbed for them.

But Trace got to them first. His hand fisted around her underwear. "They're ruined. Don't worry. I'll buy you a new pair."

She sank into her seat. Her thighs were trembling. She could still *feel* him inside of her.

Her sex kept contracting.

Her hands fumbled as she hooked the seatbelt. Skye squeezed her legs together as she tried to stop that trembling.

Very slowly, he readjusted his own clothes. He tucked her panties in his pocket. Trace kept his eyes on her. "That's the thing," he murmured.

"Wh-what thing?" Why did she have to stutter around him?

"You *are* afraid of me, but you want me anyway." His lips twisted in a smile that held no humor. "Sometimes I even wonder, do you want me *because* you fear me?"

The plane began to descend. She felt the slight change. "What kind of question is that?"

"I think you like my darkness, Skye. Because it's so damn different from what you are."

She wasn't some kind of light to his dark. She'd never seen him that way. Actually, she saw things very differently.

He should see my darkness.

"You know what I'm capable of doing." His gaze seemed to see right *into* her. "I almost killed for you when I barely knew you. And now...now you know I *would* kill for you. In an instant, with no hesitation."

She didn't want to think about what he might do. "I didn't...I didn't come looking for you because I wanted you to kill someone." That wasn't who she was.

"Are you sure about that?" he asked, and there was doubt in his deep voice. "Are you very, very sure? Think about it, Skye. Just what is it you want me to do to this man who is after you?"

The plane bumped a bit. Her hands clamped down on the armrests. "I want him stopped. I don't want him dead."

"If he was the one who caused your wreck, if he tried to kill *you*...do you truly believe I'd just turn him over to the cops?" His gaze swept over her face. "You know me better than that."

She couldn't speak then. Because he was right. She did know him better than that. He might look like the successful businessman, but there was a primal intensity to him. Just below the surface, waiting to break out.

He nodded. "Now you see me, and I see you."

***

Her dance studio was going to open tomorrow. Skye stood in the middle of the cavernous room, her gaze sweeping across the mirrors that cast her reflection right back at her.

No more broken glass. Trace's men had taken care of that for her. There were no flickering lights. And every time the front door opened or closed, the new alarm system gave a reassuring beep.

"Are you all done for tonight, Ms. Sullivan?"

She glanced toward Reese. Trace had insisted that Reese stay with her while she made all of her last minute prep work at the studio. And she certainly wasn't going to deny that having the guy with her had been reassuring.

Because she'd been afraid when she first stepped inside the studio.

But I won't let him make me afraid. The studio was important to her. It was her dream, her chance at having a new life.

"I'm done." She was. The floor sparkled. The barres were all in place. Her new students would come in to a perfect dance studio tomorrow.

A small start. That was her plan. To begin with a few classes and grow this place into the best damn dance studio in Chicago. She could do it.

I will do it.

She approached Reese with a determined smile. "Thanks for all of your help."

He inclined his head. "Anytime."

She had to laugh at that. "I doubt that you usually provide guard service at a dance studio."

"You're a special case for the boss. What matters to him…" Reese shrugged. "It matters to me." He glanced down at his watch. "He'll be meeting you soon."

It had been almost twelve hours since she'd last seen Trace. He'd had his work to attend to, she'd needed to see to her studio. And…

I wanted some distance.

Because he'd left her shattered after that *ride* on the plane.

She headed out with Reese. Pausing for a moment, Skye reset the alarm. Then they were outside. The night air wasn't as cool as it had been a few days before.

A quick glance around the area showed her that only Reese's car was in the parking lot. Everything was dark and still and —

Skye groaned. "I forget my bag. I'll be right back, okay?"

He grabbed her arm. "No, ma'am. That's not the way it works. I'll go back inside with you."

"You don't—"

"Boss's orders. Where you go, I go."

Right. She spun around and marched back toward the door. She unlocked the door and her fingers flew over the alarm pad. Reese was right at her back.

The door beeped when they slid inside. All of the lights turned on instantly.

"Just give me a minute!" She called over her shoulder as she rushed inside. "I left my bag—"

The lights shut off.

No, no that wasn't supposed to happen. Trace had hired electricians to fix the circuit breaker.

She spun back around. "Reese!"

Thud.

She stilled.

A groan reached her ears. Her breath choked out. "Reese?"

He didn't answer her.

She didn't move. Not a single step.

Then she heard something else. It sounded like — like water being poured out. *Water?*

"R-Reese?" She called again. The alarm hadn't sounded anymore. The system had just given that one beep when they'd gone inside.

Did we shut the door? Reese had been behind her. She'd rushed ahead, thinking he would shut the door.

Had he?

The water kept pouring around her. She took a deep, frantic breath and realized that *wasn't* water.

The acrid scent told her it was gasoline.

"No!" Skye shouted and ran forward. "Reese!" She tripped over something. Something soft and warm, and Skye careened to the floor. Her left leg twisted, and pain shot through her.

Her hands flew out. She touched a hard shoulder. Hair. "Reese?" Her fingers skimmed over his face and head, and she felt the sticky wetness of blood.

A light flickered in the darkness. A match. *"I will be the one."*

That voice chilled her.

The match flew through the air.

Then the fire ignited.

***

Trace slammed his Jag to a stop and jumped from the vehicle. His eyes were on the studio—on the horrifying orange and gold flames filling that studio.

"*Skye!*" Trace roared her name.

Reese's car was to the left. Empty. There was no sign of the other man or Skye.

Don't be in the fire. Don't.

But then he heard the faint cry of— "Help me!"

Skye's voice. Coming from the fire.

He ran for the building even as the windows shattered and glass flew out at him.

The main door was open, smoke billowing from it. He rushed inside, heading straight into the smoke.

Flames lit the scene. Skye was on the floor, coughing, and struggling to pull Reese's unconscious body toward the door.

"*Help me,*" she cried again as he looked up. Tears streamed down her face. "I-I can't get him on my own!"

Because Reese was three times her weight. The fire had circled in close to Skye's skin. Too close. Trace grabbed her around the stomach. Yanked her away from Reese.

Get Skye to safety. Get her out.

She screamed and struggled against him. "No, I have to help Reese!" But Trace just held her tighter. The fire was too close. Trying to scorch across her skin.

He ran outside with her. She was still coughing. She'd been in the smoke and fire too long.

As soon as he put her down, Skye immediately tried to run back for the building.

He grabbed her and yanked her right back. "Don't *move.*" The words were torn from him. Fear and rage beat in his blood, a deadly combination.

Her eyes swam with tears. "He'll die! We have to get him out—"

"I'll get him," he swore. "But you have to stay here." He had to know that she was safe.

Skye nodded.

He ran back to the fire. He rushed inside the building. The fire had spread even more, the greedy bitch that it was. The flames lapped just inches from Reese's feet.

He grabbed his friend. Pulled him up. Tossed him over his shoulder in a fireman's carry. *We're getting out of here.*

The breath in his lungs burned. The place was getting too hot. He took a step toward the door.

The ceiling fell down, coming right at him.

***

"No!" Skye yelled when she saw the flames burst through the top of her studio.

Trace hadn't come back out. He'd gone into the flames to get Reese.

And he just expects me to stay out here? While he faces the fire?

She couldn't do that. Not for another second. Too much time had already passed. He should have been back.

She leapt forward.

Sirens screamed behind her.

She was at the door, running inside because she was getting to Trace. Only—

He was right in front of her. *"Told you..."* Trace growled, "stay out of the fire."

He had Reese thrown over his shoulder. She and Trace ran from the building. Fire trucks streaked toward them.

Trace put Reese on the ground. Trace's clothes were smoldering as he bent over his friend. "Come on, buddy, don't do this..."

Reese started coughing.

"Hell, yes," Trace said.

An EMT jumped from the back of an ambulance and hurried toward them.

Skye glanced over her shoulder. The fire fighters were pulling out their hoses, but there wasn't much they could do to save the studio.

Fire had engulfed the place.

The EMTs strapped Reese onto a gurney. They pushed him toward the back of the waiting ambulance. One of the EMTs tried to take Skye's hand.

She pushed him away. "I'm fine." She couldn't take her gaze off that fire. The firefighters were trying to contain it so that the blaze didn't destroy the other nearby businesses. Businesses that—luckily—had been empty at this time of night.

The crackle of the flames filled her ears. Reese could have *died* in that fire. She'd been pulling him, straining with all of her strength, but she'd only been able to move him a few feet.

The fire had been so hungry. So hot. So wild.

I will be the one.

Reese could have died, because of her.

The ambulance's back doors slammed closed. The siren screamed once more as it raced away with Reese.

"What in the hell…" Trace began as he closed in on her, "happened here?"

"That's just what I wanted to know," Alex Griffin said as the detective stepped right in front of Skye, blocking her view of those terrible flames.

Alex? She hadn't even seen him arrive. But Skye glanced around the scene and saw that several police cars were there now. It looked like they were setting up some kind of perimeter.

"Ms. Sullivan," Alex continued, clearing his throat, "wanna tell me what just happened?"

A fire just happened. Can't you see it? Big, freaking huge, destroying my dreams.

"He was here." Skye barely recognized the hollow voice as her own. "He set the fire. T-tried to kill me and Reese."

And if Trace hadn't been there, the bastard might have just succeeded.

The flames rushed into the sky, lighting the night.

The smoke drifted in the air, and Skye watched her dream burn away.

***

The fire gutted the studio. It burned and burned and even the fire fighters couldn't seem to do anything to stop his flames.

Skye watched the fire.

Stared at it with lost eyes.

And he, in turn, watched her.

I had to punish you.

After what she'd done, Skye had needed to be taught a lesson.

As the smoke drifted into the air and the fire fighters finally backed up, he smiled.

He was pretty sure that Skye wouldn't be forgetting this night anytime soon.

Now you'll always think of me...the way I always think of you.

Every. Fucking. Moment.

CHAPTER SIX

"You saw no one?" Alex demanded as he paced the small interrogation room.

Interrogation.

Trace sat with his legs sprawled in front of him. The detective had been insistent that Skye come in to the station for an interview after the fire. Trace hadn't been about to let her out of his sight.

Because every time I do, something happens to her.

He could still smell the flames, probably because the damn smoke was in his clothes. The fire had singed him. When the ceiling had caved in, he'd had to dive fast and hard to the right. Another few inches, and both he and Reese would have been trapped. Dead?

His breath exhaled slowly. He *had* gotten out of those flames, and he'd carried Reese to safety.

His friend was going to be okay. But if Trace had arrived at that studio just little bit later...

"I didn't see anyone," Skye said softly. "But I heard him, pouring gasoline."

"How do you know it was gasoline?" Alex stopped pacing and narrowed his eyes on Skye.

She ran her hand through her hair. A black smudge slid across her right cheek. "The smell. It's pretty unmistakable, don't you think?"

He stared back at her.

Trace cocked his head. This was a colossal waste of his time. "Shouldn't you be out, detective, looking for the asshole who did this? From my count, that's an arson and an assault, all within a few days." *Attempted murder, more like.*

Alex's lips tightened. "You didn't *see* him?"

"The lights were out." Skye shook her head. "I only saw the flash of his match, then I heard his voice."

Trace tensed. She hadn't told him this part, not yet.

"What did he say?" Alex pushed.

"The same thing he said before." She was too pale. "I will be the one."

"You didn't recognize his voice?" Alex yanked out the chair on the opposite side of the table. He spun it around, then sat down, draping his arms over the chair's back. "He wasn't familiar to you, at all?"

"He was rasping, whispering." Her shoulders rolled. "So, no, I didn't recognize his voice. I still don't know who this guy is or why he's doing this to me."

Alex's fingers tapped against the chair. "You think he's the same man who caused your accident in New York?" Then he reached forward and opened a manila folder that was on the table. He shoved some stark, black and white photos across the table.

Photos of a totaled vehicle. Skye's car.

She was trapped there.

He looked up from those photos and found the detective's gaze on him. "While you were away on your little trip, I did some more digging," the detective said.

Good. I'm glad you're doing your job.

"I talked with a detective Fuller in New York." The detective glanced over at Skye. "He said you were sure someone had forced you off the road."

Skye nodded.

Trace pushed the photos back toward the detective. "We just talked to Fuller, too. The guy didn't buy Skye's story—"

"Because there was no evidence of anyone else at the crash scene. No paint from another car. No sign of a rear impact."

"My car…" Her voice was too cold for Trace as Skye said, "Rolled four times. It was smashed like a damn can. There were signs of impact all over the place."

"Fuller thought it was a one-vehicle accident," Alex continued. His gaze had locked on Skye's face. "I'm not Fuller. I know you're scared, and it sure looks to me like you have a reason to be."

It should look that way to fucking everyone.

"I'm guessing Weston took you to New York because he thought it might be one of your ex's, huh?" Now Alex's gaze swung back to him. "How'd that work out for you?"

"I'm running their alibis." And so far, turning up jack. So…no, it hadn't fucking worked out for him.

Alex pursed his lips and nodded. "Running their alibis…that's good." He put the photos of Skye's wrecked vehicle back inside the folder. "But what about your own alibi?" He pushed another sheet of paper toward Trace.

Trace stared down at a picture of himself. An image from a New York newspaper.

"You tend to catch attention when you go places," Alex murmured. "Guess that's the price of being so rich, huh? When you went to New York to see the ballet…Sleeping Beauty, right? Well, you were caught leaving the show early that night." Alex paused. "The date on the image…that would be the same day that Skye here had her wreck."

Skye's hand reached for that newspaper clipping. She pulled it toward her. "You were in New York? At my show?" Her head turned toward him. A faint furrow appeared between her brows. "Why didn't you tell me?"

"Oh, this isn't the first show he's caught." Again, Alex reached into that folder. "Seems that when you were performing, Trace here made a point of coming to see you dance. At least once, sometimes twice a month. He was always there for opening night, but he'd go back, to catch other performances, too."

Sonofabitch. The detective *had* been busy.

"You...you saw me dance?"

"He saw you, quite a lot." Now Alex seemed musing. "He liked to stay at the same hotel every time he went to see you...that posh place right off Fifth Avenue. I believe you both stayed there on your recent trip?"

"Who did you talk to?" Trace demanded. Because someone had been talking too fucking much. This kind of personal leak wasn't allowed in his organization. An assistant, an agent— someone was about to get his or her ass fired.

"I grew up in New York," Alex said with a shrug. "I've still got some friends there, and they helped me with my digging." His lips pursed. "Skye, you mean to tell me that you didn't know he was there, any of those times? With the two of you being such old...friends...I thought you'd—"

"I didn't know." Her voice was even colder now. Her eyes were on Trace. "*Why* didn't you tell me?"

Dammit. He didn't want to have this conversation with the detective's watchful stare on them. "Because we were over."

She flinched.

Hell. He was fucking this up. *We were over. You'd moved on. I just needed to see you.*

"He wasn't just at your dances, though." And, *again,* the cop pushed clippings aside. He extracted a final photo from that file. Another photo from the crash scene. Only this time, the wreckage was in the background. Skye was strapped in a gurney and being loaded into an ambulance.

"A reporter on the scene that night caught this shot, but his bosses were...persuaded not to run it."

She'd stilled.

"That man, right beside the EMTs, that's you, isn't it, Weston?"

Skye's breath rushed out. "You were there the night of my crash?"

Shit. He had to tread very, very carefully now. "I found your car. I called for help."

Skye shook her head. "*Why* were you there?"

"I think he was following you," Alex murmured as his brows lowered. "He'd been watching you for some time. I suspect he left that ballet early, and he waited for you to leave, too. Then he followed you."

"That's *not* what happened!" Trace snapped. He should have told her. Dammit, the minute she'd walked back into his life, he should have told her that he'd been there.

As if he could forget those moments. The pelting rain. The lightning that flew across the night sky.

The blood.

The sick, twisting fear because he could *not* get her out of the mangled mess that had been her car.

"You were the hero who saved her from death," Alex said as he gave a nod. "Both in New York, then here, in Chicago. You've saved her...what, two times in the last few days?"

Skye wasn't speaking. Her eyes were so big and wide and lost.

"Someone broke into her studio, slammed her head into the glass...then *you* appeared, just in time to play her white knight." Alex's voice was grim.

"I had a guard on her, I had —"

"Someone set her studio on fire tonight. Before the flames could get to her, *you* appeared again."

Skye jumped to her feet.

Trace didn't move. His hands had fisted. "You think I'm her stalker."

Did Skye think that, too?

"I think…" Alex began slowly as his face tensed in hard, tight lines, "that you've been obsessed with Skye Sullivan for a very long time. Since you were kids, right? That was when you put Parker Jacobs in the hospital. According to him, you did it just because you caught the two of them kissing."

Don't! Help me!

Trace forced his hands to unclench. "Parker is a fucking liar. You'd be wise not to believe a word he says."

Skye had backed away from the table. *From me.*

"And I'm supposed to believe you?" Alex's question mocked him. "I tried to get access to your military service records, but Uncle Sam has those sealed tight."

"That's the way they should be." He needed to talk to Skye. Alone. He'd get her to understand what he'd been doing.

"You're a dangerous man, Trace Weston. You went black ops within months of your deployment. Vanished during your service for nearly four years, then you burst back on the scene with connections to some of the most powerful players in the world."

He didn't talk about his service time. Never had. Never would.

"You came back, then you fixated on the one thing that had always mattered most to you." Alex's gaze cut to Skye. "You watched her, you wanted her, and you couldn't stand for anyone else to have her."

"Trace?" She barely breathed his name. "Tell me…tell me you weren't at the crash."

He didn't want to lie to her anymore.

"She wasn't hung up on you. Skye had other lovers, so you had to put a plan in place. You needed to get her vulnerable. She was the celebrity in New York, surrounded

by too many people. So you took that celebrity status away —
you took her dancing away. *You* caused that wreck."

"*What the fuck!*" Trace leapt to his feet. His chair slammed
down on the floor behind him.

"She was so hurt in the crash that she had to give up
dancing, and that was exactly what you wanted."

Trace stalked around the table, heading right for that
bastard.

Alex shoved away from his chair and stood up, fists
clenched.

"You took away the dancing because that is what originally
took her away from *you*, right? That's what Parker said. Skye
left to follow her dreams in New York. She left *you*."

"No!" Skye's denial. That sound halted Trace before he
could drive his fist into the cop's face. "It wasn't like that.
Trace was joining the military. He…he's the one who left me.
He told me to go." Her hair brushed over her shoulders as
she shook her head. "He rejected me, not the other way
around."

"Then maybe he changed his mind." Alex didn't glance
her way. "Maybe he saw so much blood and death during his
deployment that i⸱ made him want life again. Want *you*. But
he had to come up with a way of getting you back…and he
did. He made you afraid. So afraid that the only person you
could turn to for help would be—"

Trace grabbed the guy and shoved him back against the
wall. "You don't know what the hell you're saying."

"And you just assaulted an officer." Alex smiled at him
even as the door to the interrogation room flew open. Two
uniformed cops rushed in and grabbed Trace's arms. "I don't
care how damn rich you are, Weston, you're under arrest."

He could have broken free from the cops. Could have gone
right after the detective again. Instead, Trace offered the cop

his own, grim smile. "You've made a mistake, detective. A very, very serious one."

Alex straightened his shirt. "I don't think so. What I've done is keep her —" He jerked his thumb toward Skye. "Safe. I've shown her just what you really are."

The uniformed cops pulled Trace toward the door. He glanced over at Skye. "She already knows just what I am." She was the only one who knew what he was really like, deep inside.

He hated the pain he could see on her face.

The detective's fault. His gaze cut back to Alex. "Soon enough, you'll see, too."

"Is that a threat?" Alex demanded.

"More of a promise..." Then the cops forced him from the room. *You should know, detective, I always keep my promises.*

***

Her knees felt like rubber.

"You need to sit down, Skye," Alex said, speaking in a soft, soothing voice to her as he pulled out her chair once more.

"I don't want to sit down." She wanted him to stop treating her like some kind of broken bird. Skye raked a hand over her face. "It's not Trace."

"I know you don't want to believe that--"

"He *saved* me!"

Alex walked closer to her. Stopped less than a foot away. "That's what he wants you to believe. Are you so sure he wasn't at your studio *before* the fire started?"

"He wasn't! I was there, Reese was there—"

"Reese is a trained agent, yet it looks like someone got the drop on him. Someone snuck up and knocked the guy out. I'm guessing not many folks could do that, but Trace Weston, he *could*."

Trace could do anything.

He was at the wreck?

"You've got to stop seeing him with some freakin' rose colored glasses. He wanted you back, so he got you. He set up everything so that you *had* to return to him. Don't you see? He makes the threats, then he saves you from them."

This couldn't be happening. "I need to talk to him." She took a fast step toward the door.

Alex moved and blocked her path. "He's headed to booking. You can't talk to him now."

"You're not really going to arrest him!"

"Yes, I am." His lips tightened. "And I figure he'll have some fancy-ass lawyer who comes in and gets him out by morning, but you know what? That gives you tonight. A night to be safe. A night to *think* about Weston. Every moment you've spent with him. Realize who the hell he really is, and get smart. *Get away from him.* And you can stay alive." His fingers lifted and curled around her shoulders. "I'm trying to help you. You—dammit, you remind me of my sister. She was like you. Trusting the wrong man. So sure he was *right*." His eyes glinted with a wild intensity.

"Alex—"

"She was eighteen when that right man beat her to death because he didn't want any other man getting close to her. *Eighteen.* He thought Susan was his, and he wasn't going to let her go." He gave a rough shake of his head, but his hands were light on her shoulders. "I've seen the way Weston looks at you. You think that man's not obsessed? He is. And I believe he would do anything to have you."

I would kill for you. In an instant, with no hesitation. Her lips felt numb as she said, "He wouldn't hurt me."

"That's what Susan used to say, too. No matter how many times I told her otherwise…"

The interrogation room door opened again. "Captain wants to see you, Griffin," the female officer said as she stood on the threshold. "Wants you *now.*"

Alex dropped his hold on Skye. "Make sure she gets home safely, will you, Carol?"

"Of course."

He backed away from Skye. "Remember what I said, Skye. *Think* about him."

Then he was gone.

The female officer stood uncertainly in the doorway. "Um, miss, you ready for that ride?"

Her nails dug into her palms. "Where's Trace Weston?"

"Booking."

Right. That was the same thing Alex had said. Skye's gaze slid to the table. To the photograph of her crash. *He was there.* "Then, yes, I am ready to go."

***

The small apartment seemed to be closing in on her. Skye sat on the couch, unable to sleep. Two a.m., and she was wide awake.

The ticking of her clock seemed far too loud. Every second passed by so slowly. Every. Second.

She stood and strode toward her window. She couldn't *breathe* in that place. Skye threw open the window. An alarm immediately started to beep. One of the alarms that Trace had installed for her.

Skye's back teeth clenched. She stalked to the alarm pad and stopped that damn beeping.

Then, through that open window, she heard the sound of music. A fast, driving beat.

Coming from the club down on the corner of her street.

The music drove out the sound of that ticking clock.

Before she gave herself a second to think, Skye grabbed her shoes and her bag. She nearly ran from her apartment and down the stairs. Her legs pumped. Her left calf twinged.

Then she was outside. A line of people snaked around the side of that club, waiting to get inside.

Laughter, voices, and music drifted on the wind.

She wanted to get close to that music. She needed it.

No, not the music.

She slipped into the line.

She needed to *dance*. Dancing always helped her to forget the most painful moments of her life. Dancing helped her to cope. To survive.

She'd go in the club. She'd dance. She'd be like everyone else for a time.

I'll forget.

Because if she didn't forget, for at least a little while, Skye thought she might just go crazy.

***

"It looks like the lady's going clubbing," Carol Jones said as she settled back into her car. An unmarked vehicle, it blended pretty well on the busy street. Friday night in Chicago. Sure, it was after two a.m., but the city usually just got pumping at this time.

She tightened her hold on the phone. "She's going into the club alone." What was the name of that place? The neon letters were flashing. *Extreme.* "It's a place called Extreme."

She sure hoped that she wasn't given orders to go in that club.

Not my scene.

The beat of the music was already giving her a headache.

She'd rather take traffic duty over this detail any day.

But, if she had to follow orders…

Carol sighed. She'd do her job.

***

"Your detective made a serious mistake, captain!" Trace's lawyer snapped as he grabbed his briefcase. "He deliberately provoked my client and —"

"The charges have been dropped, Guthrie, what more do you want?" The captain, older, with gray shooting through his red hair, sighed. "Mr. Weston is free to go."

Alex Griffin stood at the captain's side.

Trace had no doubt that Alex had been ripped a new one by the captain. *You shouldn't have gone after me.*

The charges might be dropped, but the situation between Alex and Trace was a long way from over.

"Where's Skye?" Trace asked quietly.

Alex's features tightened. "She went home."

"By herself?" He swore. "Dammit, I'm not the threat to her. Someone else is out there, and you just let her go —"

"Officer Carol Jones is keeping an eye on her." It was the captain who spoke. "Carol took her home, and then we gave orders for Carol to stay and keep watch on Ms. Sullivan's place."

His racing heart calmed a bit. The cops hadn't completely screwed up.

Not yet.

"That's good to know." He jerked his head toward Craig Guthrie. "Let's go. I've seen enough of this station to last a fucking lifetime."

Guthrie nodded. The guy was on retainer. Five minutes after Trace had called him, Guthrie had rushed into the station.

The lawyer had been threatening a law suit even as the door swung closed behind him.

But, by then, the charges had already been dropped.

Alex was jerking me around.

The detective should know better than to play out of his league.

Trace's hands slammed into the main door and sent it flying open as he hurried outside. He needed to get to Skye and—

"I don't know who the girl is," Guthrie said as he grabbed Trace's arm. "But with the cops involved, it might be wise to back off a bit."

Trace paused. He glanced over his shoulder, looking back at the station's entrance. Alex had followed him out.

Not surprising.

"Backing off isn't an option," he said and he shook off Guthrie's hold. His gaze met Alex's. "Not a *fucking chance.*"

***

The club was packed.

Lights flew over the crowd even as the music pumped out from the stage.

At first, Skye didn't move.

Her gaze swept the club.

Some women wore short and low-cut dresses. They writhed on the dance floor.

Others were dressed like Skye—snug jeans, loose tops.

The music kept blaring. The beat was hard, driving.

A blond guy headed toward Skye. "Want to dance?" He had to yell to be heard over that pounding music.

Skye nodded. Dancing. It was what she needed. The only thing.

Trace lied. He lied.

She took the blond's hand.

Then she went onto the dance floor. She stopped thinking. Started feeling the beat.

And, finally, finally, stopped hurting.

CHAPTER SEVEN

The fucking asshole had his hands all over Skye.

Trace stood a few feet from the dance floor. His eyes had found Skye the instant that he stepped inside the club.

He could always find her.

Some blond jerk had his hands on Skye's hips. Skye was undulating and moving fluidly to the beat of the music.

Sensual temptation.

She pulled away from the man. Danced toward the center of the floor.

Spun. Rolled her body.

Another partner grabbed her.

She met his moves. Danced. Danced.

Pulled away.

Went to another damn partner.

The music's tempo increased. Skye easily matched the beat.

There was no limping. No stumbling. Just grace. Temptation.

No one else could dance like Skye.

Her body curved and spun. Dipped. Twisted.

Temptation.

Another partner. The crowd was loud. The band blasting.

Skye had nearly died that night. She should have been at home. Safe.

Another partner. Another. Fucking. Partner.

Trace stalked forward. Pushed his way through the crowd.

When she spun again, he was the one to catch her and pull her close.

Skye didn't even look up at him.

Her body was rocking to the beat. Moving, moving...

"Are you drunk?" Trace growled out the words.

Her head jerked toward him. She stopped dancing and seemed to finally *see* him.

Fear flashed in her eyes.

The band cranked their song up even louder.

Skye pulled away from him. Found another partner.

He followed her. "Taken," Trace snapped to the blond.

The man wisely stepped back.

"No," Skye fired right back at him. "I'm not. Leave me alone, Trace. Get out of here."

She didn't sound drunk. She sounded angry and afraid, but her words hadn't slurred.

He frowned down at her. "What are you doing?"

Skye laughed. "Dancing. It's what I do, right? The only thing..." She tried to break away again.

Not happening.

"Someone is after you!" He pulled her closer. She was still moving. Her hips undulating. "You should be home."

Her lashes shielded her eyes. "Are you the one after me?"

"Skye..."

"You're the only one I've ever counted on. Don't do this to me, Trace." Her lashes lifted. There were fucking *tears* in her eyes. "Don't be the one hurting me."

Right there, on that dance floor, with that too-loud music and the hot press of bodies, she broke him.

His hands tunneled in her hair. He tipped her head back. "I'm not, baby. I'm *not*." He kissed her. Hard and deep and desperately.

Skye had kept him sane for years, and she didn't even know it. Skye had made life worth living for him.

She thought he'd hurt her? Terrorize her?

No. Hell, no.

"Trust me," he breathed the words against her lips. "It's not me."

He needed to get her out of that club. To some place quiet so that they could talk.

He could explain then.

She stared up at him. "I love you."

The words were a punch to his chest.

"I never stopped," she said, lips trembling. "I couldn't."

To Skye, love was trust. He knew that. Because he knew *her.*

He pulled her close—and he got her the hell out of that club.

***

"She's leaving," Carol said into her phone as she watched Skye rush out of the club. "And she's not alone." Carol straightened in her seat. "Wow, wait—wasn't he supposed to be in jail?" Because that guy holding Skye Sullivan's hand sure looked like Trace Weston to her.

The man was pretty unmistakable.

She thought the couple would head back toward Skye's apartment. They didn't. Weston bundled her up in his black Jag and he raced away with her moments later.

The guy never glanced Carol's way. He'd been focused only on Skye.

Carol listened to her orders as her hold tightened on the phone. "On it, sir." She tossed her phone to the side and cranked up her vehicle.

She was supposed to keep her eyes on Skye Sullivan.

That was exactly what she'd do.

***

The elevator doors slid closed behind Trace, and he was finally able to take a deep breath as they headed up to his penthouse.

Vanilla. Skye's scent wrapped around him.

He glanced at her. She'd retreated to the back corner of the elevator. The walls were mirrored, and his stark reflection stared back at him.

He looked too dangerous. Too wild.

Story of his life.

"Why were you in New York those times?" Skye asked him.

The elevator silently rose.

He closed the distance between them. Didn't touch her. Instead, he put his hands on the mirror, positioning them on either side of Skye's shoulders. "Because I had to see you."

"Y-you could have told me. Called me—"

"Have you ever wanted something so badly…" Trace whispered as he bent his head, "that you couldn't think about anything else? All you feel is need. An endless desire that churns through you."

She gave a little nod. "That's how I feel…for you."

She was exposing her soul for him. He could do no less for her.

"And that's the way I feel for you," Trace told her. "Nothing else matters. Just *you.*"

The elevator kept rising.

"When you were eighteen, you had your dreams. Your dancing." She'd wanted her stage so badly. "For once, *once,* I did the right thing."

Her scent was making him light-headed.

"I let you go," he rasped. "It tore my heart out, but I let you go because I wanted you to be happy."

She shook her head. "Trace—"

"I had nothing to offer you. Barely two hundred bucks to my name. And you were amazing. Fucking amazing. I'd seen you dance, so many times. I knew that you'd light up those stages." He wanted her mouth beneath his. "But I also knew…you'd give all of that up, for me, in an instant."

Because, at eighteen, she'd loved him.

Skye's love had been real and wonderful and so pure. No hesitations. No limits.

Her love had been the most precious thing in his life.

She had been the most precious thing. And because he did love her, he'd tried, for once—not to be a selfish bastard.

"I didn't want you giving up anything for me. So I told you I was done. That I wanted out." When he'd just wanted her. "I hurt you." Fuck, that knowledge still tore him up. "And even as I did it, I swore to myself that I would never hurt you again."

The elevator had stopped.

"I wanted you to have your dreams. I stepped back. And I pushed you away." Then he'd gone out and clawed his way to the top. Done anything necessary to make a success of his life.

For her.

In case she ever came back to him. In case she ever gave him a second chance.

"I kept thinking you'd find someone else. Some nice, safe guy. Have a family." But she hadn't. "The years passed, and I…I had to see you. Just to make sure you were all right. Just to…fill the fucking hole in my chest from where my heart used to be."

The elevator doors opened.

"I saw you dance," he said, staring into her eyes, "and I remembered what it was like to be loved by you. To be happy."

Her lips parted. "That night…"

"I didn't cause the crash. I was…dammit, I was waiting at your place for you. I'd decided that I was going to talk to you that night. To see if you still felt *anything* for me." But the hours had passed, and she hadn't appeared. He'd gone looking for her.

And found the wreckage.

"You were awake when I found you," he said. Awake but…

Afraid. Of me. No matter what he'd said, she'd screamed and pulled away. He'd thought…*she doesn't want me anymore. She can't handle the darkness in me any longer.*

He'd made sure she got to the hospital. He'd forced his way inside to see her, again and again.

Then he'd tried to give her time to heal.

"When you walked into my office a few days ago…" He stepped back and put up his hand to keep the elevator door from closing. "I was so damn stunned. It was all I could do not to run and grab you, to hold you tight." *And never let go.*

She was still in the corner.

"I didn't burn your studio, Skye. I've always wanted you to have your dreams. I wouldn't destroy them."

Her gaze held his.

He offered his hand to her. "If you love me, you trust me."

Because that was who she was.

Skye glanced down at his hand.

He didn't move. This moment was hers.

"I don't want any secrets between us," she told him, her voice soft. "Not ever again."

He didn't let his expression alter. "Baby, you don't need to know the things I've done." Sometimes, he wanted to forget them, but his nightmares wouldn't let him.

She stepped from the corner. Moved toward him. "You're wrong. I want to know all of you." Her shoulders squared. "And I want you to know all of me." She took his hand.

Hell, *yes.*

Trace pulled her into his arms. Kissed her. He lifted her up, holding her easily. He nearly broke down the door to the penthouse before they got inside.

He didn't make it past the foyer.

Too frantic. Too desperate.

He *needed* her.

His clothes still smelled of smoke. The specter of death hovered too close.

He stripped her there. Shed his own clothes in an instant.

He took her against the wall. Driving deep and hard and sinking into the only paradise he'd ever known.

Paradise, with her.

He couldn't get inside her deep enough. Couldn't touch her enough. Couldn't kiss her enough.

With her, Trace knew he could never have his fill. He'd always want more with her. He'd want everything.

She came around him, her delicate inner muscles squeezing hard. Her release brought on his own, and his body shuddered as the pleasure pierced him to his core.

But he didn't let her go.

Didn't stop thrusting.

He couldn't. He was starving, insane with need—for her.

He'd wanted her for ten long years. She was back. No one and nothing would ever take her away from him again.

***

The phone call came just before dawn. Trace threw out his hand, grabbing for his phone.

His first thought…*Reese.* He'd been told his friend was stable. *Be okay, be—*

"Weston," he barked into the phone. If that was the hospital…

"There's a gentleman in the lobby, sir," he recognized the voice of John Ford, his building manager. "He's insisting on seeing you."

"I don't take visitors," he said, rolling from the bed. "Especially not this damn early." Ford should know better. Skye slept on, undisturbed. "Tell him to get lost—"

"He's very adamant," John's voice was hushed. "He said to tell you...his name's Mitch Loxley, and the news he has is urgent."

Loxley.

"Keep him there," Trace ordered as his gaze slid over Skye once more. *That SOB was in town? Right after the fire?* "I'm on my way down."

The sheets pooled around her body. She looked relaxed, at peace.

She'd stay that way.

He grabbed his clothes. Three minutes later, he was dressed and in the lobby.

John turned toward him. Mitch Loxley was at the man's side. Mitch appeared pale, and there were dark circles under his eyes.

What the hell does he want?

"Thank you for seeing me," Mitch began as he ran a hand over his face. "I wasn't honest with you in New York. There's...there's something you need to know."

***

"Trace?" Skye reached for him when she woke up.

But the bed was empty. The sheets beside her felt cool.

She searched the penthouse.

Trace wasn't there.

Uneasiness settled within her as she dressed.

Then she slipped from the penthouse and made her way downstairs.

***

Trace's gaze cut to John. "We need to use your office." Because he wasn't taking this guy anywhere near Skye.

John instantly nodded. "Of course! Right this way."

Trace didn't speak again, not until he and Mitch were in John's office. The building manager hurried out of the room, then shut the door, making sure to give them privacy.

Trace crossed his arms over his chest and glared at the doctor. "Your timing is shit, doc." Especially right after the fire. To be in same city…

"I had to come." Mitch paced around the small confines of the office. "I needed to tell you — ah, dammit, *you have to know the truth about her.*"

"I know plenty about Skye." He didn't need this guy cluing him in to anything.

"Really?" Mitch spun back around to face him. "Then I suppose you know all about her mother? You know that Skye's mother was psychotic? Delusional? The car wreck that killed Skye's parents…her mother *caused* that wreck. She deliberately killed herself and her husband."

Trace didn't let his expression change. "How do you know that?" Trace knew, he'd found the truth long ago, but why had this guy dug into Skye's past?

"I know because I was worried about her." Mitch blew out a hard breath. "Skye…she's too fragile. Too damn breakable."

"That's why you fucked her?" Trace demanded, voice sharp. "Because she's *breakable?*"

Mitch flushed. "I thought she needed me. Skye does something to a guy. She makes you think — she made me want to protect her."

Trace had always wanted to keep her safe.

"But...something's wrong with her."

It took all of his strength not to lunge at the doctor.

"I started to suspect the truth, after a few weeks. The things she would say, what she would do..." Mitch's hands drove into the pockets of his coat. "I talked to the detective up in New York. Fuller. *No one* pushed Skye's car off the road. I think she drove it off herself."

Bullshit.

"Skye told me about someone breaking into her apartment back in New York, she told me that she felt like she'd been watched—she told me everything..." Loxley's words trailed away.

"But you didn't believe her," Trace finished, disgusted.

"*Because it wasn't happening.* I would be with her on the street, when she was so sure someone was behind her. No one was ever there. No one ever broke into her apartment. *Nothing happened.*" A muscle jerked along his jaw. "Her mother was in her early twenties when her schizophrenia first presented itself."

Fuck. "You went into her mother's medical records."

"Delusions," Mitch muttered. "Paranoia. That's how it began for her mother—and how it begins for dozens of others. And that's how it's beginning for Skye."

No, it wasn't. "You're wrong. Someone is after Skye. She was attacked at her studio. She got a concussion—"

"Did anyone see the attack?"

No, his agent had found no one at the scene.

Mitch shook his head. "How do you know she didn't do it to herself?"

Because I know Skye. You damn well don't. "A fire nearly killed her tonight. Are you seriously standing here, trying to tell me that she might have done that, too? That she torched her own place?"

"Did anyone see her attacker there?"

Trace didn't answer.

"I thought so." Loxley's breath heaved out. "You think I want this to happen? To *her?* I don't. I *care* about Skye. But her behavior was becoming increasingly erratic back in New York. When I told her that she needed help...that's when she fled."

Trace studied the man for a moment in silence, then demanded, "Why didn't you say something when I questioned you at the hospital?"

"Because I wanted to be wrong! I wanted to be, but my gut told me I wasn't. I came here, heard about the fire just a little while ago on the news—and I *knew* that I had to see you. I had to warn you." He whirled away and strode toward the window on the right. "Believe me or don't, but you've been warned. I think—I think Skye can be dangerous. As dangerous as her mother was."

Trace kept his eyes on Loxley's back. "She didn't just leave because you tried to get her 'help'." He wasn't buying that line. "When we were in New York..." And this had been bothering him... "You mentioned something about 'that night'—how it all changed then." He waited a beat and said, "Do you really think Skye didn't tell me about what happened?" Lying was easy for him. Especially when he was facing someone like Mitch Loxley.

The doctor's shoulders stiffened. "No." He sighed out the word. "I figured she had." He turned to face Trace once more. "But doesn't that just prove my point? She confused the two of us. She called me by your name. She thought I *was* you. For an instant, Skye didn't know who I was—or even where she was."

She called me by your name.

"No one is stalking Skye," Mitch continued, his voice strengthening. "She's a severely troubled woman. Just like her mother. She needs an evaluation, medical treatment—"

"*I'm not crazy.*"

John hadn't locked the door. Shit.

Skye must have been eavesdropping outside. She'd just shoved the door open. She stood on the threshold now, chest heaving, cheeks stained red. "I'm not *imagining* what is happening to me!"

Mitch's whole body jerked, like a puppet on a tight string. "I-I didn't mean for you to hear this—"

"Obviously, but I did hear it." She licked her lips and her chin notched up into the air. "Someone is after me, and it's not some figment of my imagination. What's happening to me is real."

Mitch eased toward her. His voice was low and soothing as he said, "I know you think it is…"

"Yeah, I do! Because it's real!" She shoved her hair back. Pointed at him. "You want to talk about that night? Fine. Let's talk. I called you by Trace's name *because I was thinking of him.* I wanted him, okay? I always think of him. Every lover—it's him. That's wrong and confused, and, maybe even a little crazy, but I *know* what I'm doing. I wanted him that night, so I called for him." She shook her head. "I didn't do it because I'm having a breakdown! I did it because I wanted *him.*"

Mitch's face had turned stone. "No one can find any evidence of your stalker. Not the cops in New York. What about the ones here? I'm betting they can't, either. Even Weston Securities has turned up nothing because he's not real. Just like your mother, you're—"

"Don't talk about my mother." Her voice trembled with pain.

That was it for Trace. He leapt forward. Grabbed Mitch's arm and jerked the guy toward the door.

"Wait!" Mitch squealed. "What are you doing? Stop—"

"Get your ass on a plane, and get out of Chicago. If you aren't gone by noon, I'll know. Then I'll come after you." Trace glared into the doctor's eyes. "You don't want that, got me?"

Mitch swallowed. "I-I just want her to get help." He cast a worried glance toward Skye. She'd backed away from the door. "I care about you. I want to *help* you."

"How? By getting me committed?" Red still stained her cheeks and her eyes glinted with fury. "The stalking is real. *He* is real."

"No." Mitch sounded sad and certain. "He's not."

Trace took immense pleasure in throwing the doc's ass out of the building.

"Uh, sir…" John began as he watched Mitch storm off down the street.

"He doesn't get past the door," Trace ordered. "Not ever again, got it?"

John quickly nodded. "Indeed. I've…got it."

"Good." He strode back to the office—and found that Skye hadn't moved. Her gaze was on the window. "Skye…"

She glanced over at him. "Go talk to Reese. He can tell you that someone else was in that studio. I'm not crazy."

"I never said you were."

Her smile held an edge of sadness. "But do you wonder?"

He took her hands in his. "No, I don't."

She flinched. "I thought you were better at lying." Then Skye pulled away from him. "I thought you were much better…"

***

"I only saw Skye…" Reese shifted restlessly in the hospital bed, a bandage taped around the left-side of his head. "I felt like someone whacked me with a baseball bat, but I didn't see anyone but her."

Dammit. Trace had been hoping for more. "You didn't hear anyone?"

"If I had, the asshole wouldn't have gotten the drop on me." Reese exhaled slowly. "Skye went in the studio first. I think she forgot her bag. I can remember her going in..." His fingers clenched around the white sheets. "Then not a damn thing until I woke up in this place."

Trace put his hand on Reese's shoulder. "It's okay. You just rest."

"You got me out, didn't you? I heard the doctors talking..."

Trace nodded. "I wasn't going to leave you to the fire."

Reese gave him a tired smile. "Does that make three times...or four...that you've saved my life?"

"Doesn't matter. I stopped counting long ago." He squeezed Reese's shoulder and slipped away from the bed. "Get some rest, man."

"Wait..."

Trace glanced back at him.

"I do think...I remember one more thing." His eyes became slits as he seemed to struggle with the memory. "Your girl, telling me she was sorry...again and again. I swear, I can hear her saying that." He squeezed his eyes shut. "But that doesn't make any damn sense. Probably just the drugs they gave me."

"Probably," Trace murmured. "I'll check back on you soon."

Trace shut the door behind him.

Skye caught sight of him, and she hurried toward him. "Was Reese awake? Did you talk to him?"

He'd gone in alone because he'd wanted to gauge Reese's responses for himself. He'd also thought Reese might speak a little more freely if they were alone.

I remember one more thing. Your girl, telling me she was sorry…again and again.

"Did he remember anyone else being there?"

Trace shook his head.

Her face fell.

He *had* to ask her. "Baby, during the fire, did you tell Reese that you were sorry?"

Her fingers twisted her purse strap. "Yes."

Fuck. "*Why?*"

Her gaze flashed up to meet his. Anger lit her green eyes. "Because I wasn't strong enough to get him out of the fire! Because I was using every bit of my strength, and I couldn't get him out of there!" Her voice rose, catching the attention of two nearby nurses. "Because no matter what I did, I couldn't get him out of the door, and I was sure that we were both going to die in those flames."

He stepped toward her.

She jerked back. "But that's not what you thought, is it?" All of the heat left her voice. "I'm not crazy and you—" Sadness tightened her face. "You don't trust me."

"Yes, I fucking do."

But she'd already rushed toward the elevator. Swearing he ran after her. He threw out his hand, grabbing the doors before they could close. "I do, baby," he said again.

"This time, I'm the one who doesn't believe you." Her gaze held his. "How does that feel?"

Like shit.

"I'm going to the studio. I have to—I have to talk with the arson investigator."

"I'll come with you." He started to step into the elevator.

"No." Her clipped response stopped him.

"Skye…"

Someone else brushed by him. Maneuvered into the elevator.

"I need a break," Skye said, her voice hoarse, as if she were trying to fight tears. "Send one of your agents with me, but I need a break."

From you.

He forced himself to step back.

He held her gaze until the elevator closed.

Then Trace pulled out his phone. In less than five seconds, he had an agent ready to go. "Be her damn shadow," he ordered. "She doesn't take a step without your eyes on her."

She might want her space from him, but he wasn't about to risk her life.

CHAPTER EIGHT

It was gone. Her second chance had turned to ash.

Skye stared at the charred remains of her studio. There was nothing she could salvage there. Everything was just…gone. Destroyed by the flames.

She'd already called her students. Skye had tried to reassure them that she *would* find another space.

She hadn't mentioned that she didn't have the money to rent another building.

"Are you all right?"

She glanced to the left. As soon as she'd arrived at the scene, she'd realized that Alex Griffin was there, waiting on her. He'd come straight toward her.

He watched her with a guarded expression that made her tense. "Please don't ask me if I'm about to have a breakdown." Because that was the way he was staring at her. As if she'd just shatter apart. "I promise, I'm much stronger than I look." The female cop, Carol—the one who'd given Skye a ride home the previous night—stood a few feet behind Alex.

And Skye's newest watchdog from Weston Securities, a guy named Adam Longtree, waited about ten steps to Skye's right. She'd quickly discovered that Adam was the strong and pretty much utterly silent type.

"I'm sorry about your studio," Alex said as he inclined his head toward her. "But I didn't think you were about to breakdown. I figured if you were, well, you would've done that last night."

She squared her shoulders. "Then you make one person..."

"Pardon?"

Skye blew out a hard breath. She was so seeing her dreams covered by black and gray ash. "You make one person who doesn't think I'm on the edge of some major meltdown."

His eyes had narrowed. "Did you do like I asked? Did you think about Weston—"

She had to laugh. "Trace isn't doing this to me. Hell, he thinks I'm doing it to myself." Her arms felt chilled so she roughly rubbed them. "Trace, the cop up in New York, Loxley—"

"Uh, yeah," Alex cut in, "I don't know who the hell Loxley is, but you should know that I did some more talking with Detective Fuller first thing this morning."

"You did?"

"He got another mechanic to look at the car. There was still no sign of a rear-impact collision, but this guy did find something else." Her image was reflected back in his dark sunglasses. "All of the brake fluid was gone."

"What?" The chill Skye felt got worse.

"With all the fluid gone, the car couldn't stop. That night, you were headed into the curve, and you must have tried to brake." He raked a hand through his hair. "You couldn't, and the car lost control."

It wasn't just her arms that felt chilled. Her cheeks felt the same way. "Someone sabotaged the car."

Carol Jones stepped closer.

Alex darted a glance at Carol, then he focused once more on Skye. "It certainly looks that way."

Someone had been trying to kill her, for months. "I want this to stop." What did she have to do? *What?* "I can't live this way." Being afraid. Having a constant guard—*no.*

"We'll find him," Alex said. "Don't worry."

Easy for him to say. It wasn't his life on the line.

"With the new evidence, Fuller is re-opening the investigation in New York," Alex continued. "The jackass doing this is going down."

Carol gave a hard nod.

Skye's gaze darted between the two cops — and over to Adam Longtree. She wasn't surprised to see that he had his phone out and at his ear. The guy was probably briefing Trace on this new development right then. *Trace...* Her gaze snapped back to Alex. "You think that jackass is Trace."

He didn't respond.

"It's not."

Carol whistled and rocked forward on the balls of her feet. "Having too much faith in the wrong man could be dangerous."

"Everything I do is dangerous these days." She gave Carol and Alex a curt nod. "Thanks for your help."

She started hurrying away from them. Longtree immediately fell into step with her. Her big, six-foot-plus shadow.

"Skye!"

Pausing, she glanced back at the detective's call.

"Tell me you aren't staying with him." Tension had hardened Alex's face.

"I won't tell you that." Because she wasn't planning to return to Trace then. She hadn't lied when she told Trace that she needed a break.

Does he trust me?

Because, even after everything, she trusted him. She always had.

"If you aren't going back to Weston's place, then where are you going?"

Her gaze slid to the wreckage. "To find a new studio because I am *not* going to let my dream be taken from me." She'd find a way to get the cash that she needed in order to rent another studio. *There has to be a way.* Skye wasn't going to give up. She just had to take things—

One step at a time.

That was how she'd recovered after the accident. How she'd learned to ignore the pain and just walk.

One step at a time.

***

Alex watched Skye walk away, his eyes narrowed.

"She didn't seem particularly scared to me," Carol said as she came fully to his side.

"No, she didn't."

"Seemed more pissed, judging by the look in her eyes."

He turned his head and saw that Carol's gaze was on Skye. He followed Carol's gaze and watched as Skye climbed into the passenger seat of a waiting car. Her newest guard slammed the door and then headed for the driver's side of the vehicle.

"You're sure she went home with Weston last night?" Alex asked Carol. Dammit, he'd warned Skye. Why wouldn't she take his warnings seriously? He wanted to help her.

But he was starting to think she had a death wish.

"I'm sure that's where she went. It's not easy to mistake that guy."

No, it wasn't.

"He rushed her out of the club and into that fancy car of his," Carol said. "They went to his penthouse and stayed in all night."

I warned her.

"I guess some people like the danger too much," he said, voice gruff. His sister had been that way. He'd warned her, too.

Warned her, and buried her.

Am I going to bury Skye, too?

"Want me to keep up the detail on her?" Carol asked. Her short, honey blonde hair blew in the faint breeze.

"Yeah, stay close. If you see anything suspicious, you let me know." Over her shoulder, he saw that the arson investigator was waiting to talk with him.

Like he needed the guy to tell him that the fire had been deliberately set.

That was fucking obvious.

As obvious as the fact that someone was playing a sick game with Skye Sullivan.

A game that wasn't going to end until Skye was dead.

Just like my sister.

***

This location could work.

Skye gazed around at the old fire station. Okay, sure, most people wouldn't think this place was primed to be a dance studio...

But this can happen. I can make this work.

Excitement and determination pulsed through her. She'd make this studio even better than the other one had been. She could get started right away. If she worked fast enough, hard enough, then maybe she could even have the studio up and running in three weeks, maybe two.

The building could work, so now she just had to come up with the down payment for the place. She'd already sold all of her jewelry. Her credit cards were maxed out.

But...there were a few people who owed her some favors. People like Robert. Maybe...maybe he could loan her the cash—

"I'm taking over, Adam. You can go now."

Trace's voice. She didn't stiffen. Didn't start in alarm. Right then, she was too hopeful and happy to stiffen up.

Adam's footsteps padded away, but Trace's didn't come any closer to her.

Determinedly, she glanced to the left. She found him staring at her with a hard intensity in his gaze. "I can put the mirrors there. The barres here." She gestured with her hands. "The open area in the center will be perfect for dancers' warm-ups."

His gaze didn't leave her face. That lethal intensity didn't lessen.

Skye swallowed. *I can even use the upstairs area for an apartment. That will save me money because I can get rid of my place.*

But...she'd just gotten that wonderful security system at her place. She didn't want to lose it.

"I think you should hold off on your studio," Trace said flatly.

"No." An immediate denial. She whirled to fully face him.

He wore a dark suit, one that emphasized the darkness of his hair and made his blue eyes gleam even brighter.

"Yes, Skye," he said, voice curt. "You need to slow down. Your last place was torched less than twenty-four hours ago. Don't you think that was a message? It's not safe for you to do this. You have to—"

"I have to make this work. I have to believe that I can do it."

Dancing was the only thing that had always gotten her through life.

When she danced, she became someone else. Someone stronger.

Without it...*I'm lost.*

His hands closed around her shoulders. "It's too dangerous."

"I thought I was the one doing this to myself," she snapped at him. "Isn't that the story going around now?"

"That story is bullshit." His fingers tightened on her. "You trust me, and I trust you."

Her breath caught in her throat. She wanted those words. Wanted them so badly.

She searched his eyes, wondering if he was telling her the truth...or feeding her the lie he knew she needed to hear.

***

Carol Jones gazed across the street at the old fire station. Skye Sullivan had sure been determined. She'd gone through five buildings, touring them all with her guard right at her side, before she'd stopped at this place.

"And the guard is gone," Carol murmured as she watched the fellow hurry away.

Since Trace Weston had strode into that old fire station a few moments before, the guard's departure wasn't a real big surprise.

But...Detective Griffin didn't trust Weston. He thought the man was guilty as sin.

Maybe it wasn't safe for Skye to be alone with him.

Carol eased open her car door. Then she headed swiftly across the street. Her phone was at her ear as she entered the alley. "Hey, Griffin, it's me." She didn't wait for him to respond but hurried to add, "Skye was looking for a new building to rent. She stopped at the old fire station on Ninth, and Weston just joined her."

"Are they there alone?"

"I think so. I'm going in for a closer look."

"Be careful," he warned her.

Always. Carol eased into the alley. Maybe there was a window back there that she could use for a little observation.

She tucked her phone into her pocket and took a few more steps forward.

Yes. There was a window. One covered in grime. She leaned toward the bricks, trying to ease up closer to that window so that she could see—

Someone grabbed her from behind. A rough hand closed over mouth. "You shouldn't get involved in business that doesn't concern you," a snarling voice—a *male* voice—grated in her ear.

She reacted immediately, driving her elbow back into her attacker's mid-section. He grunted and his hold eased, just for a moment. She jerked away from him. Carol grabbed for her weapon as she spun to face the man who—

He shoved a knife into her chest.

Carol's fingers squeezed the trigger, but her attacker was already lunging away from her.

Her knees hit the ground. The gun slid from her trembling fingers and fell beside her. Her blood soaked her, and Carol didn't even have the strength to scream.

***

When the gunfire blasted, Trace grabbed Skye. He pulled her against his chest and curved his body protectively around hers.

One thunderous blast…then, nothing.

He glanced over his shoulder. That gunshot had come from out back, in the alley. Trace shoved back his coat and pulled out his own weapon.

"Wh-when did you start carrying that?" Skye asked him. Her eyes looked huge—and scared.

"I always carry it. I just usually made sure you didn't see it before." Because he hadn't wanted to frighten her away. But this moment wasn't about reassuring Skye. It was about finding out what the hell was happening in that alley.

He pushed open the rear door, but he made sure to stay low. To stay covered and —

"She's hurt!" Skye's cry.

Trace had seen the woman, too. A cop in uniform sprawled on the dirty ground.

Skye tried to lunge toward the woman, but Trace kept her back. "Wait…" Because whoever had injured the cop could still be close by. Waiting to strike again.

He looked to the left. To the right.

A weak moan escaped from the woman, and, at that sound, Skye sprang away from him. She hit her knees beside the cop and reached for the knife in the woman's chest.

"Don't!" Trace ordered as he lunged forward. His left hand flew up, locking around hers. "Leave the blade in."

"What?" Skye demanded, expression shocked. "We have to help her! She's dying!"

"And she'll die faster if you pull out the knife." He'd seen attacks like this before.

"It's Carol," Skye whispered. "Carol Jones. She took me home last night."

And she'd apparently stayed around to keep an eye on Skye.

He released Skye's hand. "Call 9-1-1," he told her. "Tell them that a cop is down." They'd haul ass getting to that location then. He kept his gun in his right hand. The attacker had to be close. He wanted to break away and search for the SOB, but Carol was choking on her own blood right then.

Shit.

He tilted Carol's head. Tried to help her breathe. Blood covered her lips. Her eyes were hazy, pain-filled.

"It's going to be all right," Trace told her. He wanted the words to be true and not a fucking lie, but the killer had known exactly what he was doing when he attacked. The knife had plunged straight into her heart and...Trace leaned forward.

The bastard had twisted the blade. For maximum damage and maximum pain.

"The ambulance is coming," Skye whispered. "Help's coming, Carol. Just hold on." Skye's fingers curled around Carol's hand.

Carol's breathing seemed so ragged and loud.

That bleary gaze of hers flickered to Trace, then it darted over his shoulder.

"You saw him," Trace said.

Carol's breathing wasn't quite so loud.

Her gaze darted over his shoulder again.

"He ran that way?"

Her lips parted. She tried to speak.

"Carol?" Skye cried. "Carol?"

Carol's eyes were still open. Still looking over Trace's shoulder.

But the officer was dead.

In the distance, an ambulance's siren wailed.

Too late. Too fucking late.

He surged to his feet. Spun toward the snaking alley that Carol had been looking at in her very last moment.

You couldn't have gone far, you SOB.

"Take this," Trace told Skye. He shoved his gun into her hands. "Stay with the cop. Help's not far away."

But he wouldn't waste any more time.

"No! You need a weapon!"

He yanked out his back-up weapon from his ankle holster. "I've got it covered." Then Trace took off running down that alley even as Skye shouted his name.

Carol fired her gun. Did she hit you, asshole? Did she?

He glanced down and saw the spatter of blood drops.

She did. And I'm gonna follow your fucking trail of blood until I find you.

"Trace!" Skye yelled.

He kept running. He was ending this, before Skye was the one he found dead in a blood-soaked alley.

***

Skye stared down at Carol. The cop's eyes were closed now. Skye had closed them. Carol's face was chalk-white. Her lips stained red with blood.

The scent of blood filled Skye's nose.

Carol Jones hadn't deserved this. To die in an alley, surrounded by garbage.

To die in someone else's place. *My place.*

Skye still held tight to Carol's hand. But her gaze was on the alley. Trace was gone. He'd run after the attacker.

She didn't want Trace dying in her place.

Not Trace.

Not Reese.

Not Carol.

"Come after me!" Skye shouted. "Stop hurting the others! You let *me* be the one! Don't hurt anyone else!"

A tear leaked from her eye.

The ambulance's siren was louder.

"Let me be the one!" She called out again. "Don't hurt anyone else!"

Doors slammed. Footsteps rushed toward her. She looked up and saw Alex rushing her way. Behind him, she could see EMTs. More cops.

Alex blanched when he saw Carol.

"I'm so sorry," Skye whispered.

The EMTs pushed her out of the way.

They tried to work on Carol.

You can't save the dead.

Carol's death was on her.

Skye looked back into the alley. No sign of Trace. What would she do if her stalker turned his attention on Trace?

"Skye."

She blinked and realized that Alex was standing right in front of her. A muscle flexed in his jaw as he said, "I want you to come with me. Come with me, *now.*"

"Trace went chasing after the attacker. We-we didn't see anyone, but Trace ran down the alley—"

"I'll have men look for him." His eyes…they burned with emotion. Pain. Grief. Fury. "But it's not safe for you to be out here. Come on." He took the gun from her hand. Led her to a patrol car.

"I-I'm so sorry about Carol." Tears wanted to choke her.

Alex nodded. The pain in his eyes deepened. "So the fuck am I. She was only twenty-two. Twenty damn two."

The EMTs weren't trying to save Carol any more.

She saw the way the other cops were acting. Saw the way they were marking the area. This wasn't about saving a life for them.

It's a crime scene now.

***

The blood trail ended at the entrance to an old factory.

Trace kicked open the doors and rushed inside. His gun was up. Ready.

Dust and cobwebs covered the factory's interior.

Trace searched and searched but found nothing. *Because the bastard led me here.*

He'd led. Trace had followed. *And I left Skye alone.*

He whirled around and started racing back to Skye.

Trace had only gone about five feet when the bullet hit him.

CHAPTER NINE

Another gunshot.

When Skye heard the thundering sound, her heart stopped. Alex ran toward the blast, and she dashed after him. Rushing faster, faster and —

Trace was on the ground. Blood was all around him.

Just like Carol.

Just. Like. Carol.

"No!" Skye screamed.

Alex bent beside Trace. Backup — more cops — raced up around them.

Skye hit the ground beside Trace. *So much blood.*

"I'm...all right," Trace managed.

Her heart started to beat again.

"SOB fired from the south. Waited for me to make a target...of myself." His breath heaved out. "Bullet's still in my chest. I'll be...fine."

He'd better not be lying to her.

In his chest.

"He's...not as good," Trace managed, "with a gun...as he is...with a knife..."

Fear clawed at Skye's insides. She grabbed for Trace's hand and held tight.

Trace's gaze — not as bright, and that dimness terrified her — found Skye's. "Get her...out," he rasped to Alex. "He could...be here still..."

She wasn't leaving him. Alex tried to pull Skye away, but she just held tighter to Trace. *"I'm not leaving you."*

Cops fanned out, started searching the area.

The EMTs came and loaded Trace onto a gurney. When they put him into the back of an ambulance, Skye jumped right in with him.

So much blood.

"Rode with you...too..." Trace whispered. "After...wreck..." His fingers squeezed hers. "Didn't want to...let you go."

"I'm not letting you go."

The EMT pushed a needle into his arm.

The ambulance jostled, bouncing along the old road. The scream of the siren echoed around her.

The EMT cut away Trace's shirt, and she got a good look at the wound.

Skye stopped breathing. "You lied to me," she whispered to Trace.

"No..."

How was he still talking? Still conscious?

"Never leave...you...this won't stop..."

The EMT connected thin tubes to him. Something started to beep.

"Blood pressure's dropping!" The EMT snapped. Then he pushed Skye back.

Trace's fingers slid from hers.

You lied to me.

Because she'd seen the wound, and she knew things weren't going to be *all right* for Trace.

***

The hospital's emergency room doors flew open. The EMTs ran with the gurney, barking out orders.

Skye sprinted to keep up with them.

Doctors and nurses jumped into action, swarming that gurney.

Please, please take care of him.

Trace vanished into the ER. The doors swung shut behind him.

She stood, alone, in that narrow hallway. Staring after him. So lost.

I can't lose him again. She and Trace just found their way back to each other. This wasn't supposed to happen.

"Miss?"

She turned and saw a nurse—a brunette with hazel eyes— gazing sympathetically at her. "Miss, we're going to need you to fill out some paperwork on the patient."

Skye licked lips that were bone dry. "He's going to be okay."

The nurse's face tightened. "There's a waiting room just down the hallway. It's the second door on the left. You can take the papers there."

"He's going to be okay," Skye said again, her voice harder.

The nurse handed her the clipboard. "You may want to notify other family members…"

Trace didn't have other family members. "He only has me," Skye said. Her fingers trembled when she took the clipboard.

She walked toward the waiting room in a daze. Bodies passed her in a blur. White lab coats. Green hospital scrubs.

Someone bumped into her, right as she turned toward the waiting room.

"Sorry," a voice rasped.

That rasp…

She looked up, frowning, just as something sharp jabbed into her neck.

A needle. He shoved a needle into my neck.

The man wore a green face mask—the kind that doctors and nurses wore during surgery—but she could see his eyes—see them so perfectly.

His eyes were the last thing that she saw before everything went dark. Skye fell forward and felt his strong arms wrap around her.

***

"Skye." Saying her name was hard. So much harder than it should have been.

Trace tried to move his arms, but found that they were strapped down. His throat ached, burned, and it sure as hell seemed like someone had driven a fucking stake through his chest.

A stake…or a bullet.

"Take it easy, Weston." A familiar voice advised him. "You just came out of surgery. They took the tube out of your throat three minutes ago. Just slow the hell down, okay?"

A tube? That would explain the burn in his throat.

Trace forced his eyes to open. Again, the small act was too damn hard. But he opened them, and he locked his gaze on Detective Griffin's. *"Skye."* He said her name again because she was the only thing that mattered.

But at her name, Alex looked away.

Where is she? She'd been with him in the alley. He remembered her holding onto him. She'd been in the ambulance, too. He'd hated the look of fear in her eyes.

"We're looking for her," Alex said. His voice cracked. *Not good.* "I've got an APB out now—every cop in the city is searching for her."

Searching for her…

The machines around him began to beep frantically.

Alex hurried toward the side of the bed. "Take it easy. Jesus, man, calm down."

He couldn't be fucking serious. Trace tried to push up in the bed.

"You're bleeding again! Stop!" Alex pushed the call button for the nurse, then he locked his hands around Trace's shoulders. The detective shoved him back against the bed. "They just dug a bullet out of you. You can't go racing out of here now!"

Yes, he could. Trace had to get to Skye.

The lines on Alex's face became deeper. "We're going to find her."

How had they lost her? *How?*

Alex exhaled on a rough sigh. "She was in the hospital. I-I saw the security video just a little while ago. Some guy in a doctor's coat came up to her. He injected her with something that knocked her out. Then the cocky bastard just put her in a wheel chair and pushed her right out the doors."

No.

"No one even stopped him. Didn't ask a single damn question. He took her out the emergency exit. There were two guards there, and he just *took her.*"

The machines were shrieking now.

Two nurses ran into the room. The male nurse demanded, "What are you doing to the patient?"

The other nurse—female, a redhead—hurried toward the bed. When she got close enough, Trace grabbed her wrist. "Get me...out..."

"No, no, sir." Her brown eyes became saucer sized. "You can't leave!"

The male nurse pulled out a needle and added something to Trace's IV bag. "This will help calm you down."

No. He didn't need to be calm. *I need Skye.*

"Take it easy," the redhead told him. "You have to rest and recover."

Resting was the last thing he needed to do. He had to get out there and find Skye. "Doc...tor..."

"The doctor will come to see you soon," the redhead reassured him as Trace's fingers slid lifelessly away from her wrist. He could feel the cold touch of the drugs slipping through his veins. "Sleep..." The nurse told him.

I can't sleep. Skye needs me.

"We'll find her," Alex told him, but the cop's voice seemed far away now. "Every cop in the city has her photo. She's not just going to vanish..."

***

But she did. Skye fucking vanished.

Two days passed, and the cops didn't find her.

"He was clever," Reese said as he guided Trace into the car. They were at the hospital's exit. *Finally.* The doctors hadn't wanted him to leave the hospital.

Fuck what they wanted.

He'd tried to leave the day before, and he'd torn open his wound. Blood had spurted and the nurses had sedated him. *Again.*

"The guy kept his face averted from the cameras," Reese told him, "and he had a surgical cap and mask on the whole time."

Trace slid into the car. The fresh stitches in his chest pulled, but he ignored the pain.

He could only focus on one thing then—Skye.

Reese slid into the front seat. The car eased into traffic.

"The cops think she's already dead." Trace had heard the whispers when Alex got his updates. As soon as they'd hit

the forty-eight hour mark on Skye's abduction, the cops had
stopped looking for a live body.

"It's…it's been a long time, Trace," Reese said softly. "A lot
can happen during all those hours…"

Trace's hands fisted. He didn't want to imagine what had
happened to Skye. "She's okay." He had to think that way.
Had to think of her being alive. Because if he let the fear take
over…*I'll lose my damn mind.* "I'm going to find her." He'd
already reassigned every agent that he had.

Finding Skye was their priority. He'd been pulling the
strings and starting the search for her even when the doctors
had been sewing him back up.

Reese slanted a fast glance his way when the vehicle
stopped at a red light. "We've got eyes on the choreographer
and the doctor in NY. Both guys have been going to work,
business as usual for them."

It wasn't business as fucking usual.

"If one of them had her…the guy would still be with her."

If she's alive. Trace heard the words that Reese didn't say.

"Could just be that it's not them. Her stalker could be
anyone." Reese kept talking as he drove them through the
Chicago streets. "Some freak who saw her dance and fixated
on her."

Trace's gaze slid to the window. "I want the plane ready to
depart within the next two hours."

The car braked at another red light. "Boss, you know that
you're not clear to travel. The doctors didn't want to let you
out—"

"We're going to New York." Because that was where the
nightmare had started for Skye. "Have the plane ready."

The killer had aimed for Trace's heart with that bullet. The
bullet had missed its target, barely.

But when the SOB had taken Skye…

You cut out my fucking heart.

He wanted his heart back.

He'd get it back.

***

The handcuffs cut into Skye's wrists. She'd lost track of time again. She'd tried counting the minutes before, a little trick to try and stay sane, but it hadn't helped.

There was no light. Only a complete darkness. It was cold. So cold there in her prison.

Her wrists had stopped bleeding. She'd thought that the blood might help her slip out of the cuffs.

It hadn't.

Her lips were cracked. Broken. Her stomach ached, but at least it had stopped growling.

She hadn't eaten. Hadn't been given a drop to drink.

She'd been taken. Then…left.

Forgotten in the dark.

She'd tried yelling before. Screaming. She'd screamed until her voice had broken.

Her hands were looped around some kind of thick, metal pole. She'd kicked it and kicked it. Jerked and pulled.

Nothing.

He's just going to leave me down here. Until I starve.

It would be a slow death.

Death in darkness.

She tried to look through the dark. To see beyond it. Skye didn't want this to be her last memory.

She wanted to remember Trace.

Trace.

He'd find her, eventually. She didn't doubt that. If he'd survived that gunshot. *He had to survive. He had to.*

Trace would heal. He'd get out of the hospital. Then he would look for her.

She hated to think about what he would find.

***

"Janie, make sure that Mrs. Summer gets her medication before—"

Dr. Mitch Loxley broke off, choking.

Because Trace had just wrapped his hand around the prick's throat.

"Stop!" The nurse—Janie—sprang to her feet. "Let him go!" She grabbed for the phone. "Security—"

"Security can wait a bit, honey," Reese said as he took the phone from her. "We're just gonna have us a little chat with the doc."

Mitch's eyes bulged. "Let…me…go…"

Trace eased his hold. "Want to have the chat out here, or in your office?" His fingerprints were bright on the doc's throat.

"O-office…"

"Good choice." He let the doctor go.

Mitch spun away from him. Strode down the hall.

"Dr. Loxley?" Janie called out uncertainly.

"I've got this," Mitch snapped back.

No, the bastard didn't.

Mitch threw open his office door. Paced inside and rubbed his neck.

Trace marched after him. Reese followed. He shut the door, then put his considerable bulk in front of the exit.

"What the hell?" Mitch demanded as he spun to confront Trace. "What the freaking *hell!* How dare you come in here and assault me—"

"Her picture is gone," Trace said.

Mitch's mouth snapped closed.

"All the pictures on your desk are gone." Actually, it looked to him like the doctor was packing up his office. "Planning a trip?"

"I've got a transfer," Mitch gritted out. "I applied for it months ago after—"

"After Skye dumped you."

Mitch flushed. "I heard about her disappearance. I-I'm sorry. I hope the cops can find her soon."

Trace wanted to drive his fist into the doc's face. Again and again until he heard the smash of bones. "Seeing as how it was some *person* who took Skye, and not a figment of her imagination, I think your theory was a little off, doc." Rage seethed in Trace's words.

"My mistake." Each word seemed torn from Mitch. "I thought...I-I was wrong."

"You were." He closed in on the doctor. He didn't like Mitch Loxley. Didn't trust him. Actually, Trace wanted to rip the man apart. "I almost killed a man for Skye once."

Mitch swallowed. His eyes widened. "You did what?"

"I wasn't even aware how close I put the guy to death," Trace said as the memory rose in his head. "He was trying to rape her. I saw...and I reacted. I hit him, again and again, until Skye pulled me off him."

Sweat beaded Mitch's forehead.

"That's what I did to him," Trace murmured as he stared directly into Mitch's eyes. "So what do you *think* I'm going to do once I get my hands on the man who took her?"

Mitch backed up. "I didn't take Skye! I've been here—"

"Actually, you came back to work the day *after* Ms. Sullivan was taken," Reese said as he stood firm by the door. "We checked. We have lots of resources to do things like that."

Mitch's gaze darted toward Reese.

"She left you, and you couldn't handle that..." Trace fought to keep his voice level. He wanted to pound into Mitch, but that wasn't the plan. He had to walk a very delicate line here. Very delicate.

The doctor shook his head. "It's not me! I wanted to help her—"

"You wanted to own her. You wanted her to be yours, but she couldn't be…Skye didn't love you, and no matter what you did, you couldn't make her love you."

A fist pounded into the door. "Doctor Loxley?"

"Looks like Janie called security after all," Reese said flatly. "Some people just don't know how to follow orders."

"I didn't want to own her." Mitch shoved his hands into the pockets of his lab coat. "That was the dancer—Wolfe. He's the one who was always controlling her. Telling her when to exercise. When to go home and sleep. What to freaking eat. He wanted to control everything about her life."

Trace kept all emotion from his face. "I'm going to kill the man who took her."

Mitch tensed. His eyelids jerked.

Such a small move.

"I am going to kill him," Trace said deliberately, "because Skye wasn't his to take."

The guards had burst inside the room.

"She was never his," Trace told the doctor. "*Never.*"

***

The guards shoved Trace and Reese outside of the hospital.

"Well, that didn't go so smoothly," Reese murmured as he gazed around at the hospital's parking lot. "But at least none of the damn paparazzi are here to see you get your ass thrown into the street."

"The meeting went exactly as I'd hoped."

Skye wasn't his to take.

When Trace had said those words, Mitch's hands had fisted. His eyes had been tight and angry, and the man had clamped his lips together to stop himself from replying to Trace.

"The guy was angry, but that was probably because you basically accused him of being a kidnapper and a killer. And because, you know, you threatened to murder him." Reese turned toward the car. "All right, boss, we need to back off."

They weren't backing any place. "I goaded him so that the fellow would make a mistake."

Reese glanced over his shoulder. "Maybe it is the choreographer, Wolfe, maybe he's…"

"I've got two agents on Robert Wolfe. They are watching him twenty-four, seven." Just in case. "And now, you and I are going to take over the watch on Loxley." Because his gut told him to stay close to the doctor.

He'd taken her pictures away. Packed up the office.

And the man in the video—that damn grainy video that Trace had watched again and again—he'd expertly injected Skye with that needle.

No hesitation.

The man who'd killed Carol had known just where to shove his knife. Known just how to twist that blade to cause maximum damage.

A doctor would know.

Trace headed toward the back of the building.

Waited.

When Loxley rushed out of the hospital ten minutes later, Trace was still waiting.

The doctor hopped into his car.

Sped away.

"Now it's your turn to be stalked," Trace whispered.

***

Footsteps.

They tapped across the floor, coming at a slow, steady pace toward her.

Skye was on the floor. She didn't have the strength to stand any more.

My wrists are bleeding again.

The footsteps kept coming closer.

Skye didn't move. She thought that perhaps she might just be imagining that sound. For days, she'd only heard—

Her heartbeat.

Her screams.

"Who…" Skye tried to ask…*Who's there?* But she couldn't get the words out. Her throat had closed up. She couldn't even cry anymore.

"It's all right," his voice told her, whispering in the darkness. "I've got you."

Then she felt something against her lips. Something wet and cool and so wonderful. She choked at first as the water poured over her lips.

"Easy. I'm going to take care of you…"

She gulped the water. Drank and drank.

Her stomach cramped. Her throat convulsed.

The water spilled from her lips. Over her shirt.

"Open your eyes, Skye."

They were closed? She blinked and the light hit her. Too bright and hard and she couldn't see anything clearly.

He was before her. A big, hulking form. Blurry.

"I'll get you cleaned up," he promised her.

Because she was filthy and bloody.

But I'm not dead.

"I will be the one you need. The only one. I will be the one who takes care of you from now on. You don't have to worry about anyone else. No director telling you that you're eating too much, that you need to work out more, to practice more…"

Robert?

"I knew you hated that life."

She still couldn't see him clearly. Her eyes just wouldn't focus with that sudden light.

His voice was husky and low, as if he were talking to a lover.

Is that what I am to him?

"I would come and watch you dance. Not just at your shows, but during rehearsal. I knew you needed me…"

The water was gone.

She tilted her head back. Stared up at him.

"Sleeping Beauty…finally waking up to see me."

Skye shook her head. "Not…Sleeping Beauty…" His features were sharpening, coming into focus before her.

"You're my Beauty. And I'll be the one to wake you up. The one who gives you life." He'd pushed the water away. The container spilled, and water poured over the floor. "Or death."

She could see him now. Skye stared into his face. Looked straight into the eyes of a man who was crazy.

As crazy as he'd accused her of being.

"There's no going back now," Mitch Loxley told her, "I've got you."

***

The windows of the brownstone were boarded up. A giant KEEP OUT sign covered the front entrance.

"Yeah, yeah, got it," Reese said into his phone.

Trace glanced over at him. The weight of his gun pressed into Trace's side.

"The brownstone is in a cousin's name. That's why it didn't come up when we did a property search for Dr. Loxley."

Because Trace had gotten his team to look up any and all properties tied to Mitch Loxley.

But his agents had come up with nothing.

Not anymore.

Trace had known that if he got close enough, if he taunted the guy, if he pushed him far enough, Loxley would break.

But he might try to take Skye with him when he shatters.

"The cops are on their way," Reese continued, voice roughening. "We should wait—"

Trace pulled his weapon from his holster. Thunder rumbled overhead. "No, we shouldn't." Because he knew Skye was in that place. Scared. Hurt?

He was getting her the hell out of there.

I'm coming, baby, I'm coming.

CHAPTER TEN

Mitch's fingers slid over her cheek. "I was so mad at you. When you went back to him..."

She shuddered. Nausea rose in her stomach. "Don't..."

"You called me by his name. When I touched you, you called for him." His hands slid under her chin, and he shoved her head back. She hit the pole. The impact had her moaning.

"You were my Beauty, and you went to him. After all I'd done...I was the one to heal your leg. I was the one at your side when you walked. I was the one—"

"Who...made me...have the wreck?"

Her brakes...Alex had said...

The nausea deepened. Skye was afraid she'd pass out.

Mitch smiled at her. Terrified her. "It was the only way to get your attention. I couldn't see you after the shows. I tried. Again and again. Beauty needed her hero to wake her up. I was there, and you couldn't see me. I had to find a way to *make* you see me."

He was a freaking *doctor*. He shouldn't have—

"I was supposed to find you that night. Not him. He was always there. Always between us." Mitch's fingers dug into her jaw. "But not anymore. Weston is dead."

Something shut off inside of Skye at those words. She could actually feel the change sweep through her.

Her heart stopped racing.

The nausea faded.

The fear vanished.

If Trace was gone, what happened next didn't matter.

"You...killed..." Skye whispered.

"I shot him in the heart because he tried to take you away from me. That wasn't happening. That wasn't ever going to happen. You belong to me."

Mitch pulled away. Fumbled in his pocket. "I'll take the cuffs off. I'll get you cleaned up, and then we're going far away from this place. Starting over..."

And he'd said she was the crazy one.

Skye's body stayed perfectly still as he uncuffed her. She'd long since lost feeling in her fingers.

He rose. "Come on, Skye."

"I-I can't stand."

Silence. Then he reached down for her. He put his arms around her and lifted her up. "See, I can take care of you." His breath blew lightly over her cheek as he shifted her body to the right.

Her eyes closed. His scent filled her nose. Disinfectant. Death.

Skye swallowed. "I don't...want you...to take care..."

Glass shattered. She heard the sound, coming from...above them?

Mitch tried to jerk away from her.

She held him tighter. *He killed Trace.* "I want..." Skye gathered her strength. Every last bit of it, and she thrust her body fully against his. "I want you...to die..."

The weight of her body sent him falling back, and this time, his head slammed into that metal pole. The crack was loud and wonderful and so perfect to her ears.

Footsteps thundered, sounding close.

"*Skye!*"

Trace's voice.

He's dead.

She dropped to her knees. Mitch was still alive. She couldn't have that.

"Skye!"

She was still hearing Trace's voice. She'd finally gone crazy.

The voices came first. That was the way it had been with her mother.

The voices.

She liked hearing Trace's voice. Maybe being crazy wouldn't be so bad.

"Fuck, Skye!"

Hands grabbed her, yanked her away from Mitch and—

Now I smell him.

Trace's scent was rich and warm. Masculine. His arms were around her, squeezing her so tightly, and shudders racked his body.

A hallucination? It was so real and so wonderful.

"Love…you…" Skye managed to whisper.

"Baby, baby, I fucking love you! You're okay, I've got you, I've got you."

He was kissing her. Her face. Her cracked lips. Holding her so tightly.

"You're dead," she said, so sad about that. Because she'd wanted to see him again. Her Trace.

"No, no, I'm not! Skye, I'm real, and I'm right here."

She just stared into his eyes.

Fear burned in his gaze. "I'm here. Baby, baby, be here, too. Be here with me."

A groan came from behind her. Mitch. She hadn't finished killing him.

The image of Trace shook her. "I found you. You're going home with me. You're going to dance, and we're going to fuck and laugh and be happy. Do you understand? Do you—"

"No," Mitch's voice. Snarling. "You're not!"

She was thrown across the room. Ripped from the arms of her beautiful hallucination and tossed to the floor.

She'd used all of her strength. Skye couldn't rise.

More footsteps were thundering. Again, coming from upstairs?

Then Skye realized…A basement. She was in a basement.

Her hands flattened on the hard floor. Pinpricks shot through her numb fingers.

"You're done." Trace lifted a gun. Pointed it right at Mitch. "You'll never hurt her again."

Mitch laughed. *Laughed.* "You're the one who hurts her. I keep her safe. I love her—" He lunged forward. There was a knife in his hand. The blade gleamed as it sliced right toward Trace's chest.

Not a hallucination. That's Trace. I could smell him. I could touch him. That's Trace.

She pushed to her knees. "No!" Skye tried to surge forward.

The bullet erupted from Trace's gun. It drove into Mitch's chest. But Mitch didn't stop his attack. He swiped out with his knife.

Trace fired again.

The knife sank into Trace's shoulder.

Trace fired. Again and again.

The knife dropped from Mitch's fingers.

Before Mitch could fall, Trace grabbed his bloody shirt-front. "I told you what would happen."

A gurgle came from Mitch's lips.

Reese burst into the room.

Trace shoved Mitch away from him. The doctor hit the floor. His eyes were closed. Blood covered him.

Skye was still on her hands and knees. She wanted to move toward Trace, but her body wouldn't listen to her. She couldn't move. *"Trace!"*

He lifted her into his arms. Held her close against his heart. "I'm here. I've got you."

She wanted to cry, but couldn't.

Wanted to scream, but her voice was gone.

She could only shake and shudder in his arms. *Trace. Trace.*

"Let me get her," Reese said, coming close to them. "You're injured...you shouldn't..."

"I've got her," was all Trace said. He carried her up the stairs.

Carried her through the old, dusted interior of a house. Then they were outside. Rain was falling. It pelted down on her, and it felt so clean. Good.

Not as good as Trace's arms.

He stood there, in the rain, just holding her. Police cruisers raced to the scene. An ambulance braked to a squealing stop.

Trace held her.

Alive.

Hope came back to her.

And her tears mixed with the rain.

***

Flowers covered the hospital room. Bright, vibrant colors. Enough petals to fill a florist shop.

The smell was heady.

The sight was gorgeous.

Skye wanted to get the hell out of there.

She'd been pumped with an IV for way too long. She wanted freedom. She wanted —

The hospital door opened. Trace stood there. The lines near his eyes were a little deeper. His face was grimmer than it had been when she first walked into his Chicago office.

His eyes were different, too. Still as blue. Still as bright.

But now she could see the love there. He wasn't hiding that from her any longer.

"Ready to go?"

She was more than ready.

He pushed a wheel chair into the room. "Your chariot."

Her brows climbed.

"They won't let you go without it. But don't worry, Reese is waiting right outside for us." He lifted her. Let his hands linger as he pressed a gentle kiss to her lips. "This place will be a memory soon." He eased her into the chair.

Trace started to push her toward the door.

She caught his hand. "What happens next?"

He bent near her, putting their eyes on level. "I take you to our suite at the hotel. I fuck you until some of this damn fear leaves me." His gaze searched hers. "Then I spend the next fifty years making you as happy as I can."

"Fifty years," she whispered. "That's a long time."

"Not long enough. I figure it's just a start for us."

He pushed her into the hallway. She couldn't help but tense. *I'll always hate hospitals.*

"I'm with you."

He knew, of course. There were no secrets between them. Why should there be?

The sunlight was bright outside. Reese waited, as promised, standing beside the vehicle.

"You look good, Ms. Sullivan," he said giving her a quick nod.

Considering that the last time he'd seen her, Skye knew she'd looked like death, so, well, anything should be an improvement over that. "Thank you, Reese. You look good, too."

He winked.

Trace eased her into the car. Buckled her seat belt. Took her hand in his.

Reese drove them away from the hospital. Skye didn't look back.

"Just so you know…we found out that Mitch's alibis were, of course, bullshit. He'd been getting interns to cover for him, and threatening to have them kicked out of the hospital if they didn't do exactly as he ordered."

"He liked control," Skye said. Control over his interns…*control over me.*

The car slowed. Turned right.

"My agents did more digging. They found out that Mitch Loxley had a history of…getting too close to some of his patients. That was why Dr. Loxley worked in five different hospitals since his residency. He liked having women…need him."

I will be the one you need. The only one.

"He said he saw me dance." Sleeping Beauty. A helpless victim, until she woke.

"He can't ever hurt you again," Trace promised. His fingers tightened around hers. "No more fear, Skye, it's over."

She didn't speak while Reese drove. Too much emotion had built within her.

When they got to the hotel, they were immediately ushered up to their suite.

It was both familiar and foreign to her.

She walked to the window. Gazed down at the busy street.

Trace's hands curled around her shoulders. "Tell me what I can do. Tell me what I need to do so that you can forget."

His voice was ragged, rough, and when he turned her toward him, she saw that his mask had fallen away.

They were alone, and she was seeing him as he truly was.

Fear and anger were in his eyes. So much fear.

He wanted her to forget, but she couldn't. Wouldn't.

She'd never forget the days of darkness and hunger. Fear. *Terror.*

But the starvation hadn't broken her.

Mitch hadn't broken her.

The thought of Trace, dying—*that broke me.*

He was the one thing that could destroy her. "I want you to love me," she told him, her voice breaking.

His mouth found hers. Trace kissed her hard and deep and she could taste his desire. "I do," he said against her lips. "I always have."

When she kissed him, she tasted the salt of her tears. She never wanted to think of a world without Trace. "I want you to be mine." She needed that, needed him, and the force of that need scared her.

He slid to his knees before her.

Trace...he never bowed before anyone. He—

He pulled a discrete white box from his pocket. Opened it. The diamond blazed up at her. "And I want you to be mine. Tell me that you will be, Skye. Always."

"Always," she said as a smile curved her lips. The first smile she'd had since coming out of the darkness.

He slid the ring on her hand, but he didn't rise. He stared up at her. "You've been the only thing that mattered to me since I was seventeen years old."

The ring fit her perfectly. So bright, the diamond sparkled.

A light, after the darkness.

"I don't ever want to be without you again," Trace told her. "Never."

Since he wouldn't rise for her, Skye sank down on the lush carpet with him. Her hands lifted and curled around his neck. "I've loved you since I was fifteen." So simple and true. "And I'll love you for the rest of my life."

They had years ahead of them. Time to laugh and fight. To have a family. To watch their children grow.

Time to just be together.

They didn't need to think about death or fear.

Hope.

Trace had brought it back to her.

She'd fight like hell to make sure that she never lost it—or him—again. She wasn't going to be someone's victim. She'd fought the monster. They both had. They'd won.

We deserve our happiness.

Skye kissed him. His arms pulled her close. Held her against his heart.

They deserved happiness, and they'd damn well take it.

This day.

And every day that came in the future. They'd survived, and now, it was their turn to be happy.

Forever.

Coming in September 2013...Skye and Trace's story will continue in MINE TO KEEP.

AUTHOR'S NOTE

Thank you for taking the time to read MINE TO TAKE. I hope that you enjoyed the story. If you would like to learn more about my work, please visit http://www.cynthiaeden.com.

HER WORKS

E-book only titles

- BOUND IN DEATH
- BLEED FOR ME
- FOREVER BOUND (A Vampire & Werewolf Romance Anthology that includes the following titles: BOUND BY BLOOD, BOUND IN DARKESSS, BOUND IN SIN and BOUND BY THE NIGHT)

Please note: All of the BOUND stories are also available separately:

- BOUND BY BLOOD
- BOUND IN DARKNESS
- BOUND IN SIN
- BOUND BY THE NIGHT

List of Cynthia Eden's romantic suspense titles:

- DIE FOR ME
- DEADLY FEAR
- DEADLY HEAT
- DEADLY LIES
- ALPHA ONE
- GUARDIAN RANGER

List of Cynthia Eden's paranormal romance titles:

- THE WOLF WITHIN
- HOWL FOR IT
- ANGEL OF DARKNESS (Fallen, Book 1)
- ANGEL BETRAYED (Fallen, Book 2)
- ANGEL IN CHAINS (Fallen, Book 3)
- AVENGING ANGEL (Fallen, Book 4)
- NEVER CRY WOLF
- ETERNAL HUNTER (Night Watch, Book 1)
- I'LL BE SLAYING YOU (Night Watch, Book 2)
- ETERNAL FLAME (Night Watch, Book 3)
- HOTTER AFTER MIDNIGHT (Midnight, Book 1)
- MIDNIGHT SINS (Midnight, Book 2)
- MIDNIGHT'S MASTER (Midnight, Book 3)
- IMMORTAL DANGER
- WHEN HE WAS BAD (anthology)
- EVERLASTING BAD BOYS (anthology)
- BELONG TO THE NIGHT (anthology)

ABOUT THE AUTHOR

New York Times and *USA Today* best-selling author Cynthia Eden has written over twenty-five novels and novellas. She was named as a 2013 RITA® finalist for her paranormal romance, ANGEL IN CHAINS, and, in 2011, Cynthia Eden was a RITA finalist for her romantic suspense, DEADLY FEAR.

Cynthia is a southern girl who loves horror movies, chocolate, and happy endings. More information about Cynthia and her books may be found at: http://www.cynthiaeden.com or on her Facebook page at: http://www.facebook.com/cynthiaedenfanpage. Cynthia is also on Twitter at http://www.twitter.com/cynthiaeden.

16578043R00094

Printed in Great Britain
by Amazon